The Equation c

Sheila Storey

First published in paperback 2020 by Sheila Storey
Publishing

Copyright © 2020 Sheila Storey

ISBN 9798673534649

The Equation of Beauty

1

London 1970

It was all the fault of my cousin Pete. Fault is the wrong word. It implies wrongdoing or blame. That Pete was the cause, the source, the unwitting originator, is a better way of expressing it. Because it was he who caused me to encounter Brennas Silvatori. And Brennas was the Alpha and the Omega of everything that was to happen.

Tall, broad, with a sheet of copper-coloured hair, reaching to his shoulders with a matching beard, he was nicknamed "the Viking", some friends calling him Vike for short. It was easy to imagine him in a horned helmet and raised axe barging across the landscape but I came to learn that picture of him wasn't true.

He seemed at first to be as mad and as enigmatic as his name. Whenever anyone asked him about the origin of his name, Brennas Silvatori, he would give a different story every time, each one being as fantastical as the name itself. Sometimes he would say that he was named after Saint Brennas, a Celt, who was a fellow monk of Saint Cuthbert in the Kingdom of Northumbria. The people who had asked the question would nod and say, "Oh yes, of course, Saint Brennas." He would tell stories about the miracles that Saint Brennas had performed, the visions he'd been granted, how he was renowned at the time for his piety and how towards the end of his life he had become a devout hermit living in the grounds of a monastery. He would tell these tales as if he himself were somehow endowed with the same qualities by dint of sharing the name and that the glory reflected on Brennas himself. However, there was no Saint Brennas. There had never been a Saint Brennas and there never would be because he was the only person with that name and when I first met him he didn't seem to be in line for canonisation.

Or he would say that he was named after Brenas, a place in southern France because that was where he was originally from. He would add that he was adopted as a baby by an English couple and so had lived in England all his life apart from those few months when he'd been French. He even mentioned that they'd added the letter n to his name so that it'd be pronounced Brennas and not Breenas, when anglicised.

It was surprising that he hadn't invented Viking ancestry to go with his looks, especially as "Brennas" had a Nordic feel about it. As for his surname, Silvatori, he would sometimes say that it was Italian and sometimes say that it was Greek. There were other stories about his name too and you could only admire his creativity whilst at the same time wondering why he was so secretive about his origins. Was it just one of his games?

The first time I met him was at my Great Uncle Robert's funeral. Great Uncle Robert was 98 when he died, all his old friends and work colleagues having already disappeared long before. There were only a few remnants of his life present at the funeral; a handful of relatives, old neighbours, and a group of people from the Care Home where he'd been living for quite some time. A room at the local pub had been booked for a little reception after the funeral for the people who'd taken the trouble to send old Robert on his way. Brennas was there and as I had never seen him before I couldn't work out who he could be. At the reception after the funeral I was standing next to him at the buffet and thanked him for coming. I asked him what his connection was to Mr. Robinson (i.e. my Great Uncle Robert) and he gave himself away or so I thought.

"I've known Norman for quite a while." He said. "We'd just sit and chat, although I suppose I should put that in the past tense now that he's gone. Lovely man."

My Great Uncle Robert's name was, in fact, Norman Robert Robinson but he'd been known as Robert since the day he was born, never Norman. The only time his full name had been displayed was on his Birth Certificate and his Death Certificate and in the obituary column of the local paper. I was aware that some people would read obituary columns in newspapers and then turn up at the funeral with just enough information from the obituary to appear to have a right to be there. It might mention where the person had worked or a particular charity that they had supported. At this point I considered getting my cousin to show this free-loader the door but I was intrigued. Why was this man so hungry that he had to crash a funeral in order to eat? I said, sarcastically, that it was nice to know that Great Uncle Robert had a friend who he could chat to, especially as he was extremely hard of hearing. It must have been quite difficult for him and difficult for you too, I'd said nodding to Brennas, trying to have a conversation with someone who was stone deaf.

"Robert?" asked Brennas.

I let rip and said something like,

"Your Norman was my great uncle and was known as Robert all his life, very deaf so didn't like being spoken to, in fact had never liked talking to anyone very much, ever, and I've never heard him described as "lovely" because he wasn't. In fact, he was quite nasty, always had been."

Brennas looked shocked, deflated and resistant somehow all at once.

"What's all this about?" I'd asked. "You obviously didn't know him at all but you're in here eating the food at his funeral. So, basically you're stealing. Shall I call the police or just get my cousin to throw you out?"

I didn't mean any of that because I have to admit that I was still intrigued. Also, I wasn't sure whether my cousin, big though he was, could have got him out.

"So why are you gate-crashing a funeral?"

I felt that he owed me and I wanted an explanation. I was on a roll and pleased with myself for uncovering his deception. I remember the conversation. Brennas said,

"Norman Robert Robinson was what was written on his door. I always spoke to him as Mr. Robinson but if I had to refer to him I would say Norman in Room 6."

"Do you mean you knew him from the Care Home?"

"Yes, sorry, I'm the Chaplain there, not a thief stealing your food."

He laughed and clearly didn't mind the accusation.

I couldn't have described the embarrassment that I felt because it was horribly indescribable. But for some unknown reason I still forged ahead.

"You don't look like a priest."

"I don't call myself a priest, that's for the Papists. I'm a Minister."

"What flavour are you?"

He looked at me, smiling, "Flavour?"

"What denomination are you?"

"Oh, you know, the usual."

He smiled and said that it was time for him to go. Despite being embarrassed by having accused him of stealing I still felt that there was something not quite right. What was the "usual" in the way of denominations? Did he mean Church of England? Was that "the usual?" As it was 1970 and so much had changed during the 1960s I supposed that I shouldn't have been surprised that a Minister had fairly long hair- all the men did in those days. He didn't dress like a Minister either but, by the same token, traditions were breaking down and people were going their own way, no longer stifled by what was supposedly expected of them. No, it was something else but I couldn't quite put my finger on it. Just intuition.

After Brennas left the funeral reception I looked through the window and noticed him talking to my cousin, Pete, the very one whom I'd been going to use as a Bouncer against him. They obviously knew each other very well, laughing and clapping each other on the shoulder. When my cousin Pete came back in I asked him who the young man was that he'd been talking to outside.

"Just now? That was Brennas. Brennas Silvatori. Grand name isn't it? He gets called Vike sometimes."

I stared at him, "Vike?"

"Because he looks like a Viking, obviously."

I ignored that and pursued my interrogation. I asked him how he knew this Brennas.

"We used to play football at the Youth Centre years ago, then he moved away but we kept in touch. He sometimes came with me to the Care Home to see Granddad. He's back up here for some reason so I asked him to come over so we could have a catch-up. It was the only chance we'd have had to meet up because he's not here for long."

"He doesn't look much like a priest, does he?" I said.

Pete gave me an odd look.

"No he doesn't. But why should he?"

"Because he said that he was the Chaplain at the Care Home where your Granddad was."

"What?" screeched Pete and burst out laughing.

I didn't find it funny and just stood there staring at him.

"That's a new one. He's never pulled that one before." Pete spluttered.

"What's that supposed to mean?" I asked.

"He's a clown. He just makes stuff up for a laugh, that's all."

"I'm not laughing."

"Hey, lighten up, Eve."

"He's not a clown, he's a liar. Why didn't he just tell me that he was there because he knew you?"

"He doesn't do any harm. It just amuses him. He only does it to people who deserve it. When he plays these tricks on people it's only ever on people who are arrogant or overbearing. It's his way of putting people down; people who need putting down. Oh, I don't mean that you're like that – I don't know why he said that to you."

But I knew why. I'd been accusing him of free-loading and coming across pretty pleased with myself for apparently finding him out. I knew I was one of those people who deserved it.

2

Providence is sometimes confused with coincidence. I've always thought that there are two kinds of coincidence. At the beginning of such events we don't know which kind of coincidence we are dealing with – is it just a pleasing serendipity or can we hear wheels turning and feel a breath on our cheek? If so, do we know if it's the waft of an angel's wing or the sniff of sulphur? One kind of coincidence is just happenstance; a converging of two events by chance and ultimately turning out to be of no import. Providence, on the other hand, I considered to be that deliberate orchestration by some higher power that can see a reason, perhaps even a long way off into the future, as to why certain energies should be enabled to meet. I'd once read it described as "synchrodestiny" and that I felt seemed to sum it up.

The coincidence that befell me after the funeral was too profound and life-changing to be given the name "coincidence". Coincidence sounds too casual, unplanned, whereas what happened to me was so far-reaching that I can only explain it by imagining that it was Providence, in the sense of a deliberate providing. Perhaps I should use the word "orchestration" because at the beginning of such events we don't know whether it is for the good or the bad. In this world of duality and opposites there is a similar energy that works in the same way as Providence but towards different ends and by different powers; that would be the opposite of

Providence which we presume comes from goodness. Perhaps it's this opposite of Providence that crafts and creates wars, droughts, fires, famines, and plagues, made ready for the four horsemen. If Providence is divine orchestration what would we call demonic orchestration? When we notice one of these coincidences do we know which power orchestrated it, which power is on our side? Should we be wary and not presume that it's good providence, but potentially the other?

My theorising on Providence versus coincidence, divine or otherwise, was suddenly and shockingly tested. I had left the funeral, walked to the station to take the train for the long journey back to my life in London, when, as I was sitting on the train waiting for it to move off, Brennas swung himself up onto the train. What was he doing here? He was, in fact, also going back to his life in London after the funeral. I'd glanced up and seen Brennas getting on the train at the very same moment that *he* saw *me*. The same look of astonishment mixed with horror must have flashed across both our faces at the same moment. He moved down the carriage to the empty seat beside me. So, just happenstance? Surely not? No, it was the other kind. But which kind? Angels or imps? I wondered.

"May I?" he asked, nodding towards the empty seat.

Thinking it would be churlish to ask him to go and sit somewhere else I begrudgingly said,

"If you must."

"Oh, but I must", he grinned, "because your cousin, Pete, told me that I'd offended you by teasing you about being a minister."

"Teasing? Don't you mean *lying* and for no apparent reason. Couldn't you have just told me that you were a friend of Pete's and that he'd invited you?"

"I would've done if you hadn't attacked me. You were very fierce, I was just protecting myself."

He laughed again and held his hands up in a gesture of surrender. I felt a smile beginning and I knew that he was right.

"Shall we just put all that behind us?" he suggested, "and pretend that I'm a stranger who's just got on the train and is sitting next to you because there's nowhere else to sit? We then have a civilised conversation and no-one's rude, no-one's attacked and no-one pretends that he or she is the Prime Minister or a brain surgeon."

"But I might be a brain surgeon. You don't know anything about me."

"Not true. Pete told me all about you. It turns out that you and I even went to the same university, just different colleges."

This was certainly odd. It appeared that we'd lived for some years in the same town, moved to the same institution in the same city, now both lived in London but it was only on a quick trip back home to the north-east that we had actually come face to face for the first time. My cousin, Pete had said that he used to play football with him but I was sure that I'd never heard his name mentioned. You wouldn't forget a name like that. During the long journey I'd tried to find out more about him but he was clever at side-stepping direct questions either by being vague, somehow changing the subject or deflecting attention from the question and so making the conversation change tack.

By the end of the journey I knew no more about him than I'd already known before, but without realising it. It was only later when I was thinking over the journey that I realised how he'd manipulated the conversation away from himself. So did he have something to hide, I'd asked myself, or was he just averse to what he considered to be intrusive questions? Perhaps he was just manically private. However, one thing that he had done was to invite me to a club where a new up- and-coming band would be playing that evening. He said that a crowd of his friends were going and I was welcome to join them. He'd taken the spare ticket out of his wallet and handed it to me. I thanked him but had no intention of going.

I had to admit to myself that there was something attractive and compelling about him, the same fascination that I'd felt while I was berating him at the funeral. I wondered if perhaps that was why he never revealed anything about himself. It would give him that enigmatic air. His personality, though, was as huge as his body as he had a cheerfulness and a wild exuberance that could only make you smile even though he could be madly irritating. I put him out of my mind as I walked back to my flat.

*

I'd shared a flat during and after university with my old friend, Marion, who owned the flat, having been bought it by her father when she came up to London to study several years ago. Fortunately, Marion would say, her father was one of those people who believed that inheritance is of more use to the child when they actually need the money, not just when their parents happen to die. But these days she was more often than not at her boyfriend's house and I'd been left to my own devices. Marion and I had often gone out together in the evenings and weekends but her latest romance was the longest either of us had ever had and it had left me feeling lonely and in fear of becoming a recluse.

Marion was standing at the window of the flat, waiting for my return which surprised me. I thought she'd be out as usual. It turned out that she and her boyfriend had become engaged. He was going to move in with her and she was going to have to break the news to me that I'd have to move out. A third person would be one too many. Marion asked me about the funeral, even made me a cup of tea and then, looking worried and serious she told me her news.

"But why are you looking so serious. That's wonderful news."

"I'm so sorry, Eve, but we'll need the flat. I'm going to have to ask you to find somewhere else to live."

"But that will be ages away, won't it? It's not as if you'll be getting married next week."

Although certain social mores had been broken down during the nineteen-sixties, living together before marriage was still looked down upon, was still not the proper thing to do, still "wrong". It hadn't occurred to me that that was what Marion was planning to do. There was an embarrassed silence as I realised the implication of Marion's request and Marion mistook my reply for condemnation. We both spoke at the same time, both saying sorry and then both laughing.

"I'm really sorry, Eve." Marion said again which made me wonder whether she was saying sorry because she was asking me to leave or sorry that she was apparently going to "live in sin".

"No, *I'm* sorry" I'd said, "it just took me by surprise, that's all, but I'm really happy for you, honestly. I'll start looking for a new place."

"You've lived here for years. I feel really bad about this."

"Not at all. It's life. Everything changes. This is your next milestone."

Marion went back to her boyfriend and I sat for a while reeling from the problem of having to find somewhere else to live. I still wasn't on a high enough salary to rent my own place. I'd have to share again, but who with? A stranger from an advert? I decided that I couldn't sort that out on a Friday night, it would have to wait. I looked at my watch. Should I go to the club that Brennas had told me about? If anything, it would take my mind off having to find somewhere else to live. I got ready quite slowly and reluctantly. Did I really want to go? I was tired after the funeral and the long train journey but as I felt restless and unsettled I decided to go out and find the club, not looking forward to entering an unknown club on my own and hoping that I would soon spot Brennas.

3

It took me a while to adjust to the darkness and the flashing lights as I went into the club. The ear-shattering music was disorientating too and all my senses seemed to dissolve as I tried to see my way through the crowds. Beery young men pushed past me or deliberately into me, slurring dubious invitations and I decided that if I didn't see Brennas within the next two minutes I was leaving. A sudden flash of wild auburn hair caught my attention and he was by my side.

"You came!" he shouted, bending down to my ear.

He led me to a far side where a bunch of people, all hair and Mexican moustaches had managed to monopolise one of the few tables and in order to introduce me all he could do was to point down to my head and shout "Eve". They called "Hi" or raised their glasses. There was no point trying to talk through the blast of sound and Brennas went to get me a drink. After a while, with our ears ringing, there was a quietish space between the warm-up band and the headliners. At this point, one of his friends took the opportunity to regale us with Brennas' latest exploit.

"Hey, listen up everybody. You won't believe this. We were in one of those upmarket bars, you know, all glass and metal, and there was this group of toffs, investment bankers, probably, drinking champagne and being rowdy in a really annoying, sort of arrogant way. Well, Vike had been standing near them at one point and he'd overheard one of them boasting that his brother had bought a Ferrari from a dealer even though he knew he was bent but he didn't care because it was cheaper than buying it legally. He'd even mentioned his brother's name, Paul."

The group stirred and leaned in to listen but I noticed that Brennas, rather than being pleased by the story of his latest victory looked uncomfortable, as if private information was being given out.

"Later", continued the young man who was telling the story, "Vike went up to the toff and very politely said that he was a friend of his brother Paul and needed to get a message to him."

There were giggles and hoots from the listeners.

"Well, this bloke had had a good few drinks by then and didn't question how this stranger knew who he was."

The story-teller tried to suppress his laughter as he continued with the story.

"Vike introduced himself as DCI Lugner but added that it was ok, he was off duty."

The group erupted and banged on the table. Hardly able to speak for laughing, he went on,

"Vike asked the man to tip off his brother that they knew about the Ferrari and as he was a friend of Paul's he'd hate to see him get into trouble! That really calmed them down and they left! Honest, it was priceless!"

When the laughter had subsided I couldn't help asking,

"Were you a detective before or after being a priest?"

A priest? The group leaned forward again - this was going to be a good story. So who was I, this stranger with an inside story on the Viking? The band was coming on so no more talking. Brennas winked at me. I got the impression from his reaction to the telling of the Ferrari story that Brennas' little dramas were for his own satisfaction, not necessarily for public consumption. Perhaps he wasn't a dramatic show-off, but on a personal crusade. But why? This little circus certainly thought that he was their ringmaster. Although he appeared to dominate the group and they seemed to look to him for their entertainment, I felt that he was different from them, detached in a way that I found difficult to define. We stayed at the club until the end and then wandered out into the cool night, the group breaking up to go their separate ways, leaving Brennas and me walking to the tube station together.

"So you still haven't forgiven me." He said, referring to my comment about the priest.

"Was that true about the Ferrari?"

"Of course. They'd asked for it – shouting their mouths off about how clever they are."

"So you've appointed yourself as the bringer-down of the arrogant. The Arrogance- Finder- General?"

He laughed."Hey, that's great. I like it. Can I put that on my business card? Look, there's time for another drink. Come down to the Half Moon."

He didn't wait for my answer and strolled off down the road, obviously expecting me to be following. Oh well, what the hell, I thought and walked along with him. It was one of those original London pubs with brass fittings, small round tables with wrought iron legs, stained glass windows and little alcoves. It was dimly lit and had so few customers that Brennas said that something must have happened and that we must be the only ones in the country who didn't know about it.

"So, when we were on the train you mentioned that you lived in Hampstead. That's a bit posh isn't it?" he said with that irritating half smile, his challenging look.

"Well, posh or not, it won't be for much longer, I'm afraid." I told him, not rising to his challenge.

"Oh, have they found you out? No northerners need apply."

I explained about my flatmate and having to move out and find somewhere else to live. His reaction was remarkable. He started laughing and said he couldn't believe it.

So I said, "What can't you believe? That I'm posh or not posh? A northerner? That I need somewhere else to live?

Then Brennas told me the strange tale. That it was such a coincidence he just couldn't believe it. Oh no, I thought, not another so-called coincidence involving this man. What's going on? Who's working overtime – angels or imps? He went on to explain:

"I live in a house with two old friends, Nick and Steve. At about the same time that your flatmate was telling you that she needed you to find somewhere else to live, Nick was telling Steve and me that he was moving out. We were going to have to put an ad in the paper or a shop window for a third person but that's a real headache. You don't know who you're getting and even if you do cringy interviews you might still be getting an axe murderer or an acid head. So it's all yours!"

I stared at him. "But you don't know me either. Not really. I might be one of your axe murderers or a kleptomaniac, psychopath, anything."

"You're Pete's cousin and you're a fellow northerner – that's good enough for me. We northerners have got to stick together down here in this foreign land where the natives think we're all flat-capped shit-shovellers."

"But what about your other house-mate, Steve? Wouldn't he want some say?"

"I can tell you for definite that he'll be as relieved as hell that he's not going to get murdered in his bed or had up for sheltering a drug dealer."

I pondered for a moment. I'm a clean, tidy person. What would the house be like with two young men living in it? I had a vision of a week's washing-up in the sink, a filthy bathroom, dirty clothes everywhere. If I was the only one who wanted a clean house would that mean that I would be the one who'd have to clean it? He cut into my nightmare as if he could actually read my mind.

"Obviously, you'll have to come and see it. We share the cost of a cleaner every week on top of the rent but that's not much between the three of us. It'll still be lower than Hampstead so you'll be quids in."

Had he really just read my mind? I'd met him for the first time just that very morning. How can life go along in a boringly straight line for so long and then suddenly and without warning it puts up a roadwork's sign followed by another very big sign marked "DIVERSION". If you just carry on, ignoring the diversion sign and don't follow the arrows to the new route you could end up in a dead end where it's too narrow to turn round and go back. I arranged to go and see the house the following evening. We strolled back to the tube station.

"So, have you forgiven me yet for my priestly episode?" He asked.

"We'll see. You're still on trial. But I *am* grateful for the offer of a roof over my head, I must say. Unless it's another one of your tricks and I arrive at the address you've given me and it's an undertaker's or a brothel or something and it's just one of your games. You'll jump out at me and have a good laugh." I replied, still not sure whether he was being serious.

"What an excellent plan! Why didn't I think of that? You are even more devious than I am."

We arrived at the tube and headed for our respective lines.

"Until tomorrow." He called.

4

We are kinder to people who are beautiful. We give them the job when the plainer candidate has better qualifications; we presume they're good people, juries giving them the benefit of the doubt; we give them slightly nicer presents and subconsciously ascribe to them all kinds of qualities that have nothing to do with their beauty. We presume that their nature is as beautiful as their face. Centuries ago, artists worked out what created beauty and they used equations and formulae to map out their masterpieces. Years later scientists would use the same mathematical formulae to explain why some people are considered beautiful and others not. It was disillusioning to discover that beauty was just all down to mathematics and ratio.

But the following evening when I went to view Brennas and Steve's house I didn't need a protractor or a set-square to see that Steve was shockingly, excruciatingly, beautiful. It's generally considered that you can't use the word beautiful to describe a male, that you should use words like handsome or good-looking but the Golden Ratio, the equation of beauty, was outstandingly evident to anyone who saw him. The beautiful people have had no hand in their own creation. They are simply fortunate that centuries of generations have crafted their looks. For example, somewhere in Steve's ancestry an eastern European had given him his Slavic cheekbones; perhaps it was a Mediterranean tryst hundreds of years ago that had given him his black hair and deep brown eyes and possibly it was a marauding Saxon who'd given him his height and strength. Those centuries of reproduction gave us the Adonis who was now sitting in a house in Kentish Town as a twenty-four year old Englishman in the London of 1970.

That house was part of a run-down terrace not far from the main Kentish Town Road but sufficient side-streets away to feel like a little backwater in the quiet tree-lined road. There was even a small walled garden at the back of the house with a flowering cherry tree to one side. But the garden had become mostly a little heathland owing to the lack of interest, energy or time, given to the space by the various tenants over the years. Brennas showed me round the house and we came to Nick's room which would be mine if I decided to go ahead and join them. It was on the first floor and had probably been the drawing room when the house was newly built. Although it was spacious and light, having two huge sash windows, the old-fashioned décor and tired furniture gave it a sad air of transience. Brennas told me later that while he was showing me round he'd started to see the house through a stranger's eyes and realised that he'd just got used to the old house and had stopped seeing all its many faults. He'd presumed that I wouldn't want to live there and had resigned himself to composing an advert. He was more than surprised when I finally gave my verdict.

"I'd love to live here." I said.

The garden, that potential little gem, had won my heart. I thought of coming in from work on a summer's evening and sitting in a garden, so quiet and private yet so close to the city centre. I was already planning what it could look like. Being in the same house as Steve would not be a hardship either, or Brennas either for that matter.

We went downstairs and Brennas broke the news to Steve that they now had a new house-mate and the three of us sat in the kitchen to celebrate. The very next weekend I moved in. I'd known Brennas for exactly one week. An orchestration had been performed. But by angels or imps? I still didn't know.

5

On that fateful train journey back to London after the funeral, I had asked Brennas what he did for a living. He'd been vague, saying "this and that". It turned out that he was doing research into lesser known poets and had been given a commission by a publisher to write a series of books on a number of these writers. We were talking one evening, soon after my move and he admitted to being in what he called the "doldrumic middle of the venture." He'd come to a full-stop in his research and was stuck.

"I'm looking into the life and poetry of a woman who lived in the nineteenth century. She was married to Frederic Stillingfleet, you know, the Romantic poet, one of Wordsworth's group of friends but she, Adelia Stillingfleet is completely unheard of herself, apart from being the wife of somebody famous. It was when I was researching Frederic Stillingfleet's life and poetry that I discovered *her* poetry too and it's far, far better than her husband's but no-one even knew that she wrote. I was given access to the library at the manor in Surrey where they'd lived. It's owned by a Trust now and allows visitors by appointment. I suppose they were glad of my interest because when the book on Frederic, the husband, is eventually published it might bring in more visitors to the house. I couldn't wait to finish the work on the husband so I could get my teeth into *her* work. It was all there in leather-bound notebooks. I don't even know if she'd ever shown her poetry to anyone."

This was the first time that Brennas had opened up about any part of his life or spoken so seriously to me in the short time that we'd known each other. So far, I had only known the entertaining, funny, beer drinking, band loving person. The jester. Now I was surprised by the man who was passionate about poetry, a woman's poetry, no less. He went on to say that he'd badly needed a break from it in order to work out how to proceed after hitting a dead end.

"I became interested, in fact, absorbed, in absolutely anything that wasn't connected with the book. I spent my time becoming an expert on the trees and birds on Hampstead Heath, I looked into the history of some old pubs in the area, even wrote articles on them. I took a sudden interest in old churches, basically, just anything for a change and to take my mind off this dead-end. Then, of course, time was going by and I got worried that I'd been wasting all this time and the publisher would soon be breathing down my neck. There's one more clue about this poet that I haven't been able to follow up yet. They had a country house in Northumberland as well as the manor in Surrey that I've already visited. The Trust has only just acquired the place in Northumberland and I'm wondering whether there's anything up there relating to her poetry. I'll have to get in touch with them again and find out if it's open yet and just get on with it. That's the last chance."

We'd been drinking in the kitchen on what was my first Friday evening since moving in. After pouring out his worries he sat at the table, deep in thought while I watched him, wanting to know more but not wanting to disturb his contemplation. Suddenly the front door banged and Steve came in, saw us sitting at the table and joined us. I had to try hard not to just sit and gaze at him. I found his display of the equation of beauty so unsettling that I hardly knew how to behave around him. Whenever we sat together I would find myself staring at him. I hoped that he hadn't noticed but as he was a rather detached, dispassionate character it was always hard to tell what he was thinking.

"So, what's up? What are you two hatching?" He asked.

"I've just made a decision." Said Brennas. "I'm going to have a few days away to clear my head and then I'm going to go full steam ahead and get my work finished one way or another and then I can get on with my life."

"Whoa! Steady on. What've you been drinking?" Steve asked, picking up the bottle. "I think we'll have to phone for help, alert the army, get you to hospital."

"Ha bloody ha," sighed Brennas. "But the new leaf is about to be turned over or overturned or whatever it is we do with new leaves."

*

The new leaf didn't get turned over until sometime later. Spring had come in mild and hopeful bringing with it a sense of possibility. One evening I stepped out into the little garden and as I stood under the cherry tree the Dryads whispered into my ear that they would like this place to be a little haven of peace and rest in place of the weeds and rubble that denied its purpose. Brennas came out into the garden as if he, too, had heard the call wafting in the branches of the tree.

"Brennas, I'd love to make this into a proper garden. It's such a waste. Would it be ok if I started working on it? I don't have much to do at the weekends at the moment."

"What a great idea! Hey, I'm up for that." He responded.

"What about your plan? You were going to have a break and then finish your book."

"But this could be my break. I could help with the garden for a few days. It'll be an incentive. When shall we start? Let's have a look now."

He said it in a way that seemed dramatic and urgent, as if he'd found the answer but it could just have been another excuse to delay finishing his research.

As we pulled the long grass apart we found green shoots of spring plants trying to force their way through into the light. We screeched with delight as each plant was uncovered, like a couple of children on an Easter egg hunt.

"We must get all this grass out to let the sun onto these poor neglected plants." I told him as I stood up and stretched.

We hadn't noticed how dark and cold it had become so, reluctantly, we went indoors. Steve had come home in the meantime and had watched us for a while from the window. It was a curious sight, he told us, like looking at a giant and a fairy digging for buried treasure. Against Brennas' bulk, I looked even smaller than I really was. I'm short and slight with dark hair, the exact antithesis of Brennas.

"What on earth are you two doing? Have you found an unexploded bomb?" Steve asked in his bemused, slightly ironic tone. "You looked like beauty and the beast or an ogre and an elf."

"Beast? Ogre? That's no way to speak about Eve." Said Brennas.

We laughed and then I said,

"Anyway, elves are male."

Steve looked at me, mockingly. "If all elves are male how do you ever get more elves?"

"Perhaps they're created, not born, and they're immortal so you wouldn't actually need anymore." I explained to him.

Steve rolled his eyes. Brennas looked over at me and said,

"You're wasting your time. You're forgetting that Steve's an engineer – therefore - no imagination."

"At least I'm doing something that's useful to the world, not fannying about with dead poets."

"But it's literature that makes us humane, softens the heart, takes out the brute lurking inside us all, makes us civilised, for the want of a better word." Countered Brennas, stung by Steve's put-down of his work.

"We couldn't manage without my bridges and roads but we could manage without your poets." Steve retorted.

"Yes, we could manage but it would be a stark, desolate world." Sighed Brennas.

"So, Elfie, what do you think?" Steve asked me.

"Elfie?"

"Yes, you're Elfie from now on."

"To answer your question - it's an exploded garden not an unexploded bomb." I replied. "We're going to resurrect it and your engineering expertise would be welcome. You could devise a bench to go round the tree or make a path through."

I could see that Steve wasn't sure whether I meant it or whether I was making fun of him. We sat round the table with cups of tea and Steve and Brennas started their usual bickering again. This time it was about the

Beatles break-up then on to the Cup Final between Chelsea and Leeds that had ended in a draw and would need a re-play; then they argued about "True Grit" that they'd seen at the cinema the week before. I took this opportunity to study Steve. He really was astonishingly beautiful. I couldn't fault any part of him, even if I'd wanted to. In fact, he was so good-looking it hurt to look at him.

You know when someone's staring at you, even if they are behind you. You can feel it. It's an intuition that we've inherited from our cave-men ancestors to protect us from predators. Sure enough, Steve suddenly turned from Brennas and looked at me. He was too quick for me. Before I could look away I noticed that he was looking at me differently from his usual disinterest. He seemed to be appraising me as if it was the first time he'd seen me. I hadn't blushed since I was about fifteen but before he could see it I jumped up and said that they were always arguing about rubbish and it was boring so I fled to my room. I heard them laughing as I ran up the stairs.

6

I still couldn't align in my mind the Brennas who talked about bands, football and which was the best beer; the Brennas who played wild tricks on people he didn't even know; he who looked like a wild barbarian – I couldn't align him with the Brennas who was going to save from obscurity a nineteenth century woman's poetry and who spoke passionately of her feel for language, of her striking metaphors and unusual descriptions of the countryside; a woman whose gift to the world had been hidden. It was the equivalent of knowing a slender young girl in a floating chiffon dress, with gold sandals, perfect make-up and shimmering hair and then discovering that she was training to be a car mechanic. Brennas was that kind of anomaly. We don't see things like that these days but this was then, when you were placed into your appropriate slot according to what you looked like. On the other hand, perhaps that does still go on.

Brennas was true to his word, putting his time and energy into sorting out the garden. Every evening now that dusk was getting later I was able to help when I came in from work. Weekends were the best because we could spend all day weeding and digging, hauling and groaning. We'd stop for breaks every now and again, sitting on the sacks of rubble that we'd collected and have endless cups of tea. He asked me about my work at the library and seemed unusually interested although I was to find out why later. He seemed to be no longer playing the enigmatic persona with me, speaking openly about his life as we sat on the uncomfortable bags of stones. But even so, the story of his life was still strange and I couldn't help suspecting that he might still be playing games. One Saturday, I asked him about his life, his childhood, why he'd moved from the north, how he'd got his unusual name. His story was a sad one - if it was true. As my cousin Pete had told me, Brennas had lived in my old home town on Teeside where he'd been living with his grandparents. Eventually, when he was old enough, he was sent to a boarding school.

"It was a good school, the staff were kind, the kids were ok, nothing nasty but I always felt apart, sort of disjointed, unsettled. I used to wonder what it was like to live in a house with a father and mother and go off to school every day and then back home in the afternoon. My grandmother died and so during the holidays, instead of going to stay with my grandparents as usual, my grandfather arranged for me to stay with the Housemaster and his wife and their children. It was good of them but it made it worse because I saw then what a family was and I knew I wasn't part of it even though they were kind to me."

He looked worn out by the memory of it and stood up, picked up the spade and started work again. I wondered how that sad, lonely child had ended up being such a cheerful, warm person. That background would have been more believable of Steve than

Brennas. I decided to find out more but now wasn't the time.

It rained all day on the Monday of the following week so I presumed that work on the garden would have stopped for the time being. I was on the late shift at the library so I couldn't help that week as it was dark when I got home. I was bothered about how long the rain would last, putting back our plans and enabling Brennas to take even more time away from his work. On the Thursday the rain stopped and I wondered whether Brennas had started on the garden again or whether it was still too wet.

I didn't see either Brennas or Steve when I worked late as our time in the house didn't coincide. Then I was away all weekend, staying with an old friend down in Devon and I didn't return to the house until early Monday evening when, coming in from work, I discovered Brennas hard at work. He'd discovered that we weren't creating a new garden but revealing the original one. He'd uncovered a patch that had possibly been a lawn surrounding the cherry tree and two circular flower beds with old roses that were still showing signs of life. Crazy paving ran around the tree and the flower beds, none of which had been visible in the thigh-high grass that had taken possession. Steve wasn't around as much as Brennas and me and he'd taken a rather derisory view of our gardening. He had a cool, casual air of detachment which didn't have Brennas' warmth and openness. In fact Brennas would call him sullen and moody to his face but Steve would just smirk and insult Brennas back. I wondered how they'd come to share a house when they so often argued and insulted each other.

Steve was the only one of us who had a car but when we asked him if he'd take the huge bags of weeds and rubble to the tip he just laughed at us. But he did agree to lend it to us which surprised us. Getting those sacks out of the way made a huge difference but the best part was about to happen. I'd gone in to get changed so that I could help with the very last patch to be cleared when Brennas gave out a kind of yelp. He was clearing that last area of very long grass and called me over. There, lying on its side, completely hidden from view, was an old, stone bird bath. It had remained completely intact, no chips or cracks, protected for years by the overgrown plants. All it needed was to be brushed down. I ran into the house for the brush, got rid of the soil and all those bits of grass that had clung to it for years. Brennas fixed it into the middle of one of the flower beds. I filled it with water, not only for the birds to drink from but in my imagination it had mysteriously appeared like a font for the baptism of the new garden. So the the garden was finished; my little dream complete.

To his credit, Steve was surprised when he came back and he congratulated us, admitting that it had been well worth doing even though he'd doubted it at the beginning. We showed him the bird bath.

"It's a gift." I said.

Steve asked who it was from and I said that it was from the elemental nature spirits who lived in the garden. They were thanking us for what we'd done. I said this deliberately to irk Steve because I knew that he had no feel for the metaphysical. Brennas raised his eyebrows, cocked his head on one side, smiled and nodded. But Steve just rolled his eyes, tutted something about hippy rubbish and started to walk back to the house.

"Why don't you come and sit out here, Steve." I called. "You can be the garden gnome."

He stopped in mid-stride and half-turned as if to say something but then continued into the house. I'd noticed that when Steve was scowling or sullen as he often was, he was still beautiful. How could that be? If any part of an equation or ratio is distorted then surely it no longer holds true. But Steve's equation of beauty according to the ancients didn't falter in the face of frowns and down-turned lips. I decided to do a little equation of my own because if it's all about Maths we should be able to solve it but it would look like this:

If x=beauty and y=a scowl then the equation in Steve's case would still be $x - y = x$ which is nonsense. I carried on with my useless equation and came up with another one:

Let $x = B$ (for beauty)   Let y = facial distortion

$x - y = B$ therefore $y = 0$

So, in other words, Steve's beauty is so massive that nothing can take away from it, scowls being miniscule compared to the vastness of the beauty. Is that what I was trying to understand? I remembered that if I had a grumpy look on my face when I was a child, my father would say that it spoiled my beauty or if I'd been grumpy and then suddenly smiled he'd say that I looked pretty when I smiled and that I should remember that when I was feeling crotchety. So, obviously my beauty wasn't in the same league as Steve's because my facial distortions would have created a more believable equation.

I'd drifted off into this mindless miasma when Brennas suddenly broke into my thoughts and said that I should ignore Steve and not let him provoke me. He then went off down the road to get some drinks to celebrate. He was carrying the usual beers and lager, apologising for not bringing champagne which the garden surely merited. Steve had an extra sensory perception for when beer had come into the house and he came out to join us. Brennas teased him that he couldn't have a drink because he hadn't helped but we were too pleased to be mean and, sitting under the cherry tree, we raised a toast to the garden. The Dryads smiled, applauding softly from the boughs, their whispers carried off on the breeze.

We sat there for some time, not saying much, just enjoying the mild air and basking in the transformation that we'd made. I took the opportunity to ask Brennas and Steve how they knew each other. They looked at each other, Brennas laughing but Steve with a superior smirk. Brennas explained.

"We were at the same college at the University and at that point we didn't know each other. It was Freshers' Week, we'd be only eighteen or so and I'd managed to get a date with this gorgeous girl, the lovely Marion, and I couldn't believe my luck. We had a few dates but then suddenly she wouldn't see me anymore and I found out she'd gone off with another bloke."

At this point Brennas gestured towards Steve, "and there he sits."

Steve continued the story.

"I was sitting in the Refectory minding my own business when this brute", he pointed at Brennas, "came marching up to me practically telling me to come outside. But when I told him that she'd already gone off with someone else, he calmed down, we went for a drink and as it was the first week at Uni neither of us knew anyone else so we just sort of stuck together. We decided that Marion was obviously sampling all the lads until she found what she was looking for which turned out to be Nick, our ex housemate whose room you now have."

Brennas took up the story again.

"Steve and I met up with Nick later on not realising that he was the one who'd finally won the delicious Marion. When she joined us in the pub one night and Nick introduced us it was really embarrassing but looking back I suppose it was funny. But they stuck together because the reason he left here was because they're getting married."

Marion and Nick? Those names together rang a very loud bell.

"Nick's last name isn't Hewitt is it? I asked.

They both looked surprised. "You know him?"

"The reason that I needed somewhere to live was because Marion, my flat-mate, was getting married to someone called Nick Hewitt."

"Wow! So Marion, who it appears we all know, the very Marion who came here so many times we thought she was moving in, was actually *your* flat-mate and the cause of you moving in here." Brennas repeated, looking astonished.

Oh, how to describe my feelings? Providence? Coincidence? Angels? Imps? What's going on? How can such a massive Universe be such a small world? We went on sitting under the tree in a kind of stunned stupor until the soft breeze gave itself an edge and the dusk reminded us of the time. We went indoors and Steve reminded Brennas that his work on the garden was his final excuse for not getting on with finishing his next book. He reminded him that he'd called it a break that would refresh him ready for the final onslaught. Then Brennas told us his news.

"This very morning I had a letter from the Trust that owns the Stillingfleet's country house in Northumberland, Glen Hall. They said that all the papers and books from the library had been put in a repository years ago when the last member of the family died and the house had been shut up. All these things had only just been returned to the house so nothing had been gone through yet. The boxes hadn't even been opened. They've only just acquired the Hall and as they're reliant on volunteers it would've been a long time before they got round to the library. Their very words were that they would be delighted if I sorted through the papers and books for my research which would at the same time be doing them a great service." Brennas told us.

He looked so pleased that we couldn't help but applaud and wish him well.

"So when are you going?" I asked him.

"There are a few things to iron out first but it should just be in a couple of weeks. Before I do that though there's something I need your help with, if you don't mind." "What's that?" I asked him, still suspicious of him, despite knowing him a lot better now.

7

Brennas explained that years ago, when his grandmother died, her sister, his great aunt Dorothy had asked Brennas' grandfather for something that she remembered Brennas liking and that his grandmother had said that he could have. She'd remembered that he'd loved a china ornament because there was a little dog included in the group of figures. The ornament had originally been bought by his grandmother's mother so it was by now an antique. Ugly though it was, it was worth a reasonable amount of money because although it had been a cheap ornament at the time his great-grandmother had bought it, it was now a collector's item, so his great aunt had informed him. He went on with his story:

"I liked it when I was a kid but only because of the little dog. I really don't want it now and it's been lying around in my room all these years so I thought I'd see if I could sell it. I don't really need the money but I don't like having stuff around that I don't want. I like to travel light. So, I've been wandering round the streets trying to sell it to antique dealers but I don't look the part. I suppose I looked scruffy and they didn't even want me in the shop, never mind look at the thing. They probably thought I'd pinched it. So I smartened myself up."

I asked him how on earth he'd managed to do that but he ignored the comment and continued with his tale.

"As well as looking smart I put on an air of confidence and approached yet another shop. It worked because I had a different response this time. The dealer told me what it was worth, which was way more than I'd imagined, but then he said that it wasn't the kind of curio that he himself dealt in. But, he *did* give me the names of some dealers who he thought would be interested. I'm going to try them out this week. Now this is where you come in." He said looking at me. "They're real snobs these people so I'm going to smarten myself up again and apparently people are more trusting if there's a woman too and not just a man because for some unknown reason they think that women are more trustworthy and subconsciously they feel happier with a man *and* a woman in their shops because they feel safer, more normal with that sort of arrangement."

He carried on in this vein for some time until Steve interrupted.

"Get to the point, Vike. Are you asking Elfie here to be the mystery woman, the one to make you look normal?" He howled with laughter. "Nothing could make *you* look normal, mate."

Brennas didn't mind. He ignored the jibe and asked me if I'd mind dressing up and accompanying him the following Saturday. I imagined it as one of Brennas' dramas. If the dealers were arrogant and supercilious it could turn out to be very embarrassing, having watched him deal with such people before and, of course, having been at the pointed end of that myself, too. But there was that fascination again and against my better judgement I said I'd do it. Steve howled again and said he'd like to be a fly on the wall and asked,

"So are you going to be Mr. and Mrs. Silvatori or will it be Signor and Signora or whatever the Greek is for Mr. and Mrs."

"We won't have to introduce ourselves. I can introduce myself I suppose and then the dealer can just make up his own mind as to who the mystery lady is. If we get into conversation and he asks I'll just introduce Eve as .....Eve."

Steve did one of his eye rolls and pouted his mouth but the golden equation of beauty remained the same.

Brennas had the names of three antique dealers who might be interested in the delicate china group of a lady with a parasol, a gentleman, flowers, and of course, the dog. He noticed that one of the dealers had a very unusual surname and that gave him an idea. He went to the public library and did some research, tracking down a man with the same surname in "Who's Who". He presumed that as it was such an unusual name that this person in "Who's Who" must be related to that antique dealer. He memorised the Cambridge College that this man had attended and various other details including, most importantly, his date of birth, as Brennas couldn't suggest that he himself had been at University with someone who turned out to be twice his age.

We met in the kitchen on the appointed day and I was pleased with the reaction. I'd spent time trying to look the part, wearing an outfit I'd worn at a wedding, the right amount of make-up and my long hair tied up in a chignon. But Brennas was the one who stopped us in our tracks. Even Steve had to admit that Brennas had done himself more than proud. He'd managed to straighten his hair back into a low pony tail in the nape of his neck. He wore a blue shirt and dark suit. I don't think I'd have recognised him. I'd have walked past him in the street.

We got the tube to Mayfair and I became nervous. I couldn't trust Brennas' behaviour. What was my part in all of this? Was I supposed to just stand there or join in? Was I just the female appendage? I'd asked Brennas but he was vague about what I was supposed to do. He just said that he needed my presence because if he went in on his own they'd smell a rat. They'd be suspicious.

We found the shop. As we'd imagined, it was formidable. Two grand candlesticks with twisted stems stood in the window with intricate carvings of foxes and snakes and horrible unknown creatures swarming over the dull silver. There was an oil painting of a gory deer hunt and an equally revolting painting of the Rape of the Sabine Women. It was a grotesque place and I suggested that we should go to one of the others.

"He won't like your statue, it's too sweet. He obviously likes macabre, nasty things."

"No, I've done my homework. Come on." And he opened the door into the monstrous den.

Inside, it was suffocating, from another era. There were large lamps which were lit to show the pictures of miserable castles painted onto the glass shades, pottery similar in style to Brennas' and a table bearing the weight of heavy jewellery. Further back in the shop you could see dramatic furniture; huge wardrobes whose insides had witnessed the tobacco reeking clothes of some Edwardian gentleman, rocking chairs that you could imagine creaking to and fro on some overgrown, weedy veranda and some strange items clearly from the time of the Raj.

The dealer greeted us but was, as Brennas had imagined he would be, disdainful and superior. He had a short pointed nose and tiny round mouth reminding me horrifyingly of a squid. I instinctively backed away so that any sudden thrashing tentacles couldn't reach me. As the dealer inspected the statuette with turned-down lips, Brenas said,

"May I ask? You have a very unusual surname. My father was at King's with a Richard of the same name. You wouldn't be related by any chance?"

The dealer stopped looking critically at the china piece and looked up with a look of pleased astonishment.

"Well, well, Dickie, yes he's my cousin."

"I remember my father talking about him and the name, being so unusual and striking, stayed with me. I think they rowed together or played rugby or something, I forget now." Said Brennas, playing it down.

"Well, what a coincidence, young man. Yes, Dickie did more rowing than studying, I think. And what is your name?"

"Brennas Silvatoris."

Brennas told me later that he'd added an s to his name to make it sound more Greek.

"Ah yes, another unusual and striking name. Would that be the Greek Silvatoris? Met Yannis a few times. Is he still around?"

"I'm afraid we're estranged from the Greek side – some feud or other." Brennas replied casually.

"Shame", said the dealer, "Nice chap."

The dealer carried on reminiscing about dear Dickie, the Greeks, King's College which he himself had also attended at a later date, and seemed to have forgotten why we were there. He finally looked down at the china people that he'd been twirling around in his hands while he was speaking and proclaimed it to be a delightful piece, absolutely typical of its type and era, and, in fact, very popular at the moment. Brennas mentioned that it had originally been bought by his great-grandmother, then passed on to his grandmother but he himself didn't care for it and had decided to part with it. He said sweetly that he would remember his grandmother in other ways. The dealer held it up,

"Yes, *very* popular at the moment. You've decided to part with it at exactly the right moment, Mr. Silvatoris."

He offered a price even higher than the value that had been given to Brennas earlier. I could hardly breathe while the conversation was going on and I had to wander away and pretend to be interested in the hideous jewellery. Although I was nervous it was tinged with a desire to laugh and also mixed with awe at Brennas' amazing acting ability. We had to wait until we were well away from the shop before we both stopped and laughed until there was no sound and we just shook. When we'd recovered he said in a pompous voice, similar to that of the antique dealer's,

"Now Madame, as a reward for your services I'm going to treat you to lunch."

We went to a little French Bistro where he announced a second request for my services, far stranger than the first one.

*

"Do you have any holidays owing?" he asked.

I was taken aback and didn't answer. He went on.

"It would be very helpful to me if I had a librarian with me when I go up to Glen Hall in Northumberland. I told you how they are letting me run riot in their library with all these unopened boxes and I'd be really grateful if you could go through it all with me and then perhaps bring some order to it all. It wouldn't be all work though – there'd be the sea, the hills, lots of walks ………"

This was so unexpected, and to be honest, so weird, that I still didn't answer.

"Sorry." He said. "It wouldn't be much of a holiday for you, doing what you normally do all the time."

The truth was that I hadn't had a holiday for quite a long time and was owed at least a few weeks leave. Also, going through papers and books that hadn't been handled for a long time wouldn't be the same as my usual job. It would be fascinating. But could I put up with Brennas for a couple of weeks cooped up together?

"I shouldn't have asked." He said. "It was presumptuous of me. You don't know me very well and I *am* a Viking after all. But, anyway, everything would be paid for, lodgings, meals, whatever."

I couldn't help but smile.

"It was just a surprise, no, more than that, it was a big shock and I'll have to think about it. When do you need an answer?"

"They've said that they'll be ready for me in a couple of weeks."

I said that I'd let him know but I was already feeling that eye-brightening surge of excitement. To have free rein in a manor in the Northumbrian countryside, to rifle through a library untouched for years, to walk by the sea. I knew I'd go and asked for leave from the library the next day. It was the best time of year to ask for time off because being the end of June by this time, the students had mostly left the university. There was still a lot to do; administration, stocktaking and planning but I had no trouble in securing three weeks' holiday.

Later that evening when Brennas came in I asked him if he'd meant it when he'd asked for my help at Glen Hall.

"Of course I did. Why would I have asked you if I didn't mean it?" He said looking a bit hurt.

I told him that I'd got the time off and I would go. His delight was so great that he lifted me up and twirled me round, thanking me and saying how much help that would be and how much quicker it would make it. At that moment, Steve came in.

"What the hell's going on here?" He asked with his $x - y = x$ frown.

Brennas told him about our trip to Northumberland and Steve looked absolutely astounded. He gave me a very strange look that I couldn't fathom.

"You're going to help this wastrel with his book?" He asked me, in a tone of utter amazement. "How on earth did he manage to persuade you to do that? He must be paying you a hell of a lot of money to work for him."

"I'm not going to help Brennas with his book. How could I? I don't know anything about his poet. I'm just going to help to organise the papers and the books. It'll be like a holiday as well."

Steve carried on looking at me in an odd way and then put his bag down, puffed out a tut and went upstairs. I looked at Brennas questioningly but he shook his head and just said

"He's like a child."

8

Brennas had asked the Trust if he could bring a librarian with him and they were apparently overjoyed at their good fortune. I still had to send them a copy of my credentials and a reference as to my trustworthiness but after two weeks we were ready to go. During those two weeks we'd had to put up with Steve's sardonic comments and unsavoury suggestions. He seemed bemused by the whole thing. Brennas invited him to go up and see us one weekend for a break but he said he was going to savour having the house all to himself for a heavenly three weeks.

Brennas didn't have a car because he said that there was no point in having a car if you lived in London. He decided to rent one rather than suffer the long train journey and when he turned up in a Mercedes I stood at the window gaping in astonishment and said,

"Good heavens! Look at that!"

Steve stood up and came and looked. He laughed.

"That doesn't surprise me." He said. "He's filthy rich, you know. Or didn't you know?"

No, I certainly didn't know and I laughed.

"Oh yes, you can tell that just by looking at him. All those Saville Row suits he wears." I said sarcastically.

If anyone was rich it certainly wasn't Brennas.

"I'm serious. How do you think he can spend years studying dead poets that no-one's ever heard of? I doubt whether he could live off what he earns from that series he's writing."

Was Steve jealous that Brennas could dedicate himself to something that Steve considered to be useless? I then asked Steve,

"If you could spend a few years doing whatever you wanted and had enough money to do it, what would you do?"

He answered without even having to think about it.

"I'd travel."

"But you've got a good job", I said. "You could save up and take holidays wherever you wanted."

"I mean a different kind of travel; the sort where you can wander about for years all over the world."

I noticed for the first time a kind of wistfulness in those lovely eyes of his. Perhaps his cynical attitude was a just a cover to hide his real self. He did come over as unhappy sometimes, or at least, unsettled.

"Brennas could do whatever he wants and he just moulders away in this shit-heap and reads dead poetry. He's mad. The money comes from …….."

He stopped abruptly as Brennas breezed in, all energy and busyness. We were to set off early the next morning so I started to leave the room to go and pack.

"Just one thing, Eve". He called. "We'll pass close by my great aunt Dorothy's. Do you mind if we call in? Do you still have any relatives left in the north-east? We could call in on them too if you like. I know your cousin Pete's moved away now."

"No, great uncle Robert or should I say *Norman* was the last one to live there, apart from Pete and his mum." I said, harking back to the time when Brennas and I had first met.

He grinned that sheepish grin that always settled on his face whenever he was caught out or wrong-footed.

*

Steve was nowhere to be seen when we left early the next morning. Brennas left a light-hearted note for him on the kitchen table reminding him of when we'd be back so that he could get the house tidy ready for our return and have the beer ready on the table.

We were quiet for the first part of the journey as Brennas nosed his way out of the Capital, already busy so early in the morning but as we got out onto clear stretches we relaxed and talked. I wanted to find out about Steve.

"Tell me about Steve. I don't know anything about him."

"You do. You know that he's sarcastic and sullen". Brennas laughed. "You know that he's a logical robot with no finer feelings."

"That's a bit harsh." I said. "Yes, he can be like that. He can act normally and be friendly, well, friendly in his own way, and then the next minute he's all closed off. I never know how he's going to be. What's the matter with him?" I asked.

"I suppose I've just got used to him." Brennas said. "I ignore it. I just think of him as having a tantrum, like a child."

"But there must be a reason for it." I pursued. "Do you know anything about his background?"

"He only ever talks about himself when he's had a bit too much to drink."

Then Brennas glanced at me and said, "You'll have to get him drunk."

I didn't say anything and we sat in silence for a while watching the traffic building up around us. It was going to be a long journey. We didn't have a break until we got to Leicester but that was just for a quick coffee. It wasn't until we arrived in York that we had a decent break with something to eat in a little café in the shadow of the Minster. What a pity we couldn't have stayed in York all day with its narrow cobbled streets and history, but we had to plod on.

In North Yorkshire, I looked out of the car window and noticed the Howardian Hills sliding into the Hambleton Hills, the Cleveland Hills then chasing along beside us to our right and fields spread out for miles to our left. Brennas pulled off the A1 into a side road, reporting to me that we were now near Great Aunt Dorothy's. He'd warned me that it wasn't for nothing that she was called Dorothy because she could be slightly dotty.

"I don't mean she's batty, quite the reverse. She's very alert and energetic. She's just a bit eccentric, I suppose and getting forgetful too. She must be at least in her mid eighties, if not older."

We drove through lanes, dappled with sunlight filtering through the tunnel of trees until we came to a driveway on the right. There was no sign of a house until the drive curved and when the house emerged I was so shocked that I couldn't speak. A huge Art and Crafts style house stood before us, nestling into a gentle green slope behind. A circular drive at the front surrounded a grassy circle. To each side were rustic fences hiding what I imagined would be gardens equal to the house. Brennas had already parked and was getting out when he noticed that I was still sitting there, immobilised.

"We're here. Come on."

"It's beautiful." I murmured. "Why didn't you tell me? I had no idea ….."

"I'm just used to it I suppose." He said, which I realised was his response to most questions.

What had I been expecting? A post-war three bed-roomed semi? A row of terraced houses? A little cottage? I don't know, but I certainly hadn't been expecting this. Eden Manor.

We walked up to the massive oak doors just as they opened and a small, elderly lady came running out, surprisingly light on her feet. She ran up to Brennas and hugged him although she could barely reach further than his waist. Then she turned to me and very warmly took my hand and led us, still holding my hand, until we were in the huge hall and Brennas closed the door behind us.

"Mrs. Thompson! They're here!" Tea please!" she called.

We sat in the most beautiful room I had ever seen. The huge windows looked out onto a terrace and lawns, then onto the far woodlands beyond. Running along the top of the long window was a series of separate stained glass panes, each showing a bird perched on a branch, apparently singing and surrounded by a swirl of various flowers and leaves. The wallpaper seemed to be the original red, green and gold stencils of complex lilies and leaves. Plasterwork of acorns and oak leaves enhanced the edges of the ceiling. We sat on deep sofas next to little tables that Mrs. Thompson had set next to each of us for our cups of tea. I was so entranced and dumbfounded that I couldn't function for a while, trying to take in this astonishing house. Mrs. Thompson handed round a plate of cakes and biscuits and then left the room.

"Mrs. Thompson's my treasure," great aunt Dorothy said to me, "she does everything in the house and her husband does the gardens."

I noticed that she'd said gardens in the plural, not garden in the singular. It reminded me of our little patch in Kentish Town. Great aunt Dorothy leaned forward in her animated, affectionate way, embracing us in her warmth and her delight at seeing us.

"Remind me what you're doing, Brennas. You mentioned in your letter that you were coming up this way to do some research. What's that about?"

"I'm going to a house in Northumberland called Glen Hall because I'm looking into the life of Adelia Stillingfleet, the wife of Frederic Stillingfleet, the poet."

"Oh yes, that's right, I remember now. I had to remember to tell you that I met her a few times." Dottie said in a matter of fact voice.

Brennas couldn't hide his stupefaction, surely the time line was all wrong.

"I don't think that's poss......" he started. "It must have been someone else, auntie." Brennas said. "She was dead by the time you came to live here. Can you think who else it might have been?"

"No. It was her. I definitely knew her."

As a keen student of coincidence and providence I would have loved Brennas' great aunt Dorothy to have met Adelia. How neatly it would have woven into this tapestry. I tried to do some mental arithmetic to make it possible. Could they have met if Dorothy was very young and Adelia was very old? I'd need paper and pencil. Adelia's names were unusual. Could aunt Dorothy be right that they'd struck a chord? Then as if she had said nothing momentous Dottie turned to Brennas who looked as if he was in a trance and asked him if he'd mind helping Mr. Thompson move some heavy things in the garden. He went out through the French Windows in search of Mr. Thompson, and Dottie, as she insisted I call her, turned her attention fully on to me.

"I think it's wonderful that boys and girls can live together in the same house these days without being married or related in any way. In my day, we'd have been ostracised, accused of running a ménage á trois or worse. Young people can be so much freer now without disapprobation. When I was your age I was simply expected to marry, have children, run a household and my husband would be the head of that household. I was fortunate. I broke free, and what's more, I did actually avoid the disdain and rejection which I knew would be coming my way when I returned. But I suppose that Brennas has told you all about that."

I answered that actually he hadn't, that all I knew about her was that he was very fond of her. Her face lit up but just as she was about to tell me more, Brennas came back in and said that unfortunately we must be on our way.

"On your way back to London would you like to call in again? In fact, why not come for the day and then stay the night? That way, we can catch up properly."

We agreed that was a lovely idea and that we'd look forward to it. I hoped that would give me a chance to look round the whole house and garden. It was breathtaking. We set off and Brennas told me how Dottie imagining that she'd met Adelia was typical of how Dottie was sometimes literally dotty and here and there she would mix people up or she would have a memory about something that happened which was completely different from everyone else's recollection. He then told me a bit about her life, how in 1902 when she'd have been around twenty, she'd inherited a large amount of money and gone off to the continent on her own. This, of course, was absolutely not done amongst the young ladies of Dorothy's position in society. It was just presumed that if she ever returned it would be as a fallen woman, as they would call it. But she'd proved them all wrong or at least just revealed their hypocrisy.

"The story goes," continued Brennas, "that in 1914, just before the outbreak of the First World War she returned, wearing a wedding ring, very well-dressed and appearing to be extremely well-off. She told the family that she'd married a Frenchman, a lot older than herself. He was from an old aristocratic family, he being the only member of the family still alive. He'd died though after they'd been married for only a few years. The political situation was getting dangerous and she'd decided to come home. Whenever anyone asked her about her late husband she'd say that it made her too sad to talk about it. She says that she reckons that she was only accepted back into the family and their friendship circle because she was wearing a wedding ring and was wealthy. None of us ever found out the truth but I think enough time's gone by now and all the other players have died so perhaps she'll open up one day."

We were nearing the end of our journey and soon we were parking in the car park of the historic "Golden Fleece Inn" where we'd be staying. We went into the olde worlde hotel, checked in and arranged to meet up later for dinner. It was a relief to throw myself onto the soft bed and doze, dreaming of Vikings and Frenchmen, wars and mysteries. As usually happens in such cases, I had no idea where I was when I woke up and slowly took in my surroundings as a shaft of fading sunlight seeped through the latticed window, alighting on a print of Renoir's "Ball at the Moulin de la Galette." Ah yes, I remembered, the delightful Dottie, the supposed or true wife of a French Count.

The next day would prove whether Brennas was on a wild goose chase. He had no idea whether the archives at Glen Hall would yield any more information or anything at all about Adelia, her poetry or her life. All he knew was that she would go to Glen Hall alone, whenever her husband was busy in London or abroad. If she did write there, did she even keep what she had written? If so, where was it?

9

It was the big day. I'd seen pictures of Glen Hall so I knew what to expect, unlike my first view of Dottie's house. It was a relatively small Georgian country house of perfect symmetry. If you asked a child to draw a house, Glen Hall is exactly what they'd draw. The Trust's warden, Mrs. Howard, came out to meet us. She was a brisk, formal, middle-aged lady but welcoming and enthusiastic. She led us into the house and as she opened the door to the drawing room she explained that she and two volunteers would be concentrating on that room while we were in the library. She led us through all the rooms from the attics to the cellars but as everything was still swathed in drapes and with shutters still closed we couldn't see much.

She'd saved the library until last. This room was at the back of the house and it was clear to see why. Window seats ran along the length of each of the tall windows which overlooked the garden.The room was flooded with the early morning light which glanced off paintings and porcelain. Drapes had been removed from a magnificent desk and the bookshelves had clearly been cleaned ready for our arrival. Large cardboard boxes stood on the floor labelled either "Papers" or "Books". We couldn't wait. Brennas needed the desk and I needed the large table at the far end of the room under another long window. We worked in silence for hours, lost in the fascination of it all. Mrs.

Howard brought in a tray of tea which woke us from our absorption.

The books were mainly what I'd expected; poetry, Shakespeare, histories, books on nature, books on the local area, cathedrals, castles. Frederic, a lot older than Adelia had been part of Wordsworth's group of friends, spending time at Dove Cottage in Grasmere when he was a young man. To someone like myself who loved the Romantics it was an indescribable feeling to see inscriptions in the poetry books by Wordsworth himself, Coleridge and so many others with whom Frederic had spent those long-ago summers. Brennas had shown me some of Adelia's poetry and I'd had to agree that it was easily on a par with those famous Romantics. So why had she been left out? I was so absorbed that I jumped with fright when Brennas spoke.

"There are only bills for hats and dresses here and tradesmen's stuff, just paperwork to do with the house. There are no more notebooks. But not to worry, I've got a billion more boxes to go through yet. Oh, come on, let's have a break."

We went out into the gardens that surrounded the house. A group of volunteers was busy weeding and again, I thought of our little garden back in the dusty, dirty air of Kentish Town so far removed from this haven. By the end of the day we'd been through several boxes but Brennas still hadn't found anything that he could use. Not yet.

Several days went by in a blur of boxes and more boxes that were getting Brennas nowhere. I, on the other hand, had plenty to do, cataloguing the books for the Trust, making notes, finding more inscribed little volumes which I passed over to Brennas. I was in my element but Brennas was despairing, losing faith. We took the afternoon off and went for a long walk into the hills. Cool breezes roused us from our preoccupation and reclaimed us from the eighteenth and nineteenth centuries. The trail we were following rose high into the hills and when we reached the top we were rewarded with a sudden and unexpected view of the sea. We sat down and gazed at the mass of blue, flecked with white, spread along the horizon. I thought about how in one way, I now knew Brennas very well but overall, I didn't know him at all. I dared myself to ask him about his life again. For example, he never mentioned his parents. It might be a sore spot. He might resent intrusive questions. But I took the risk and plunged in head first.

"Tell me a bit more about yourself. You've mentioned your grandparents but you haven't said anything about your parents."

He was only in his mid-twenties so where were his parents? Why had he only ever mentioned grandparents? He was quiet for a moment and then turned and looked at me. He seemed to then make a decision, possibly that I was a person to whom he could tell his story.

"My grandfather came from the family that had originally started digging the iron ore out of the Cleveland Hills. They had foundries, steel mills, interests in ship building. They were the big wigs in the area. My grandparents only had one child, my mother, and much to my grandfather's horror, after the war she started seeing a man who'd been in the RAF but who, my grandfather found out, had previously worked in one of his foundries. After the war, a lot of social boundaries had dissolved but not in his world, I'm afraid. He absolutely refused to allow the marriage. What he wanted for his only child was some sort of dynastic marriage with an heir to a ship builder in Sunderland or something like that, as if he was a king joining two countries. He was a stern man and quite nasty and bad-tempered to be honest. He always had to have his own way. But, so I was told, my mother defied him, said that she'd marry my father anyway because when she was twenty-one she wouldn't need her parents' permission."

I was sitting on the top of the hill, looking at the seascape sweeping before us, utterly rapt by this story. But then I spoilt it by remembering how often Brennas had made up stories in the short time that I'd known him and perhaps this was just one of those. He didn't know what I was thinking and I didn't interrupt him to question the veracity of the story and he continued.

"So, that's what they did. As soon as they were twenty-one they went off and got married. They had me within the year but my grandfather still wouldn't relent and have anything to do with his only child and new grandchild. We'll never know whether he would've eventually come round because my mother and father were both killed."

This piece of information was given in such a conversational tone that it took me a moment to follow what he'd just said.

"Killed?" I repeated in a voice that sounded as if I didn't know the meaning of the word.

"Train crash. I was with them but I wasn't killed." He smiled. "Obviously."

I was completely hooked on the story now, whether it was true or not.

"My grandmother had taken the estrangement very badly and when they were killed she blamed my grandfather. Although she was under his thumb she somehow managed to insist that they should bring me up and he must have agreed because for the first few years of my life I lived with them. But, as soon as I was seven, though, he sent me off to his old boarding school. Grandma made sure that I came to them during the holidays and that's how I go to know your cousin Pete and his granddad, or should I say you're your great uncle *Robert*." We smiled yet again at the memory of the funeral and our unpromising first meeting.

"Quite often great aunt Dorothy would come over too and I remember those times as being really happy.

When grandma died, aunt Dorothy knew that my grandfather wouldn't be able to manage having me around during the school holidays so she offered to have me. She told me that he'd said that he didn't want me around her loose ways and that she'd never pulled the wool over *his* eyes. So he arranged with my Housemaster that I would stay with him and his family during the holidays. I think that's why I worked so hard at school. All I wanted to do was to get out and be my own person, be grown up, be free."

What could I say? If I challenged him as to whether it was true or not, it would be insensitive if it was, in fact, true. However, if he'd made the whole thing up for reasons best known to himself, I didn't want him to think that he'd got one over on me and have a laugh at me for soaking it all up. Neither of us said anything and as a cool breeze reminded us that we weren't far from the North Sea we stood up and made our way back to the Hall.

*

The very next day everything changed. I had just opened another box full of more of Adelia's books. I took them out and put them into their respective piles of Poetry, Nature, History and so on. I picked up a book on the trails and pathways of Northumbria and as I turned the pages a slip of paper floated out. I imagined that it had been used as a book mark as it was marking a page of trails that ran by the Hall. I opened the sheet of paper and the shock of what I read there made me gasp. It started "My darling, most beloved Adelia" but ended with, not Frederic, her husband's name, but "your devoted ever loving, Edward" At the top of the letter was the name Edward Wansbeck with an address close to the Hall.

"Oh, my goodness, Brennas, look at this."

I handed him the letter.

"She was having an affair!" he exploded. "I've never heard of this person, have you?"

"No, but the address is local so perhaps Mrs. Howard, the warden, might know about him."

We went into the drawing room.

"Mrs. Howard," Brennas called. "Have you ever heard of Edward Wansbeck?"

She carefully put down a particularly beautiful piece of china and came over to us.

"Oh yes, he was a local artist. He lived quite near here."

"Do you know if he ever came here? Presumably he knew the Stillingfleets."

"I imagine he did", she said, "because this place is absolutely full of his paintings."

"Really? Would it be possible to see any of them?" Brennas asked.

"All the paintings are waiting in the dining room. They've been unwrapped so you're welcome to go in and see them."

We thanked her and set off for the dining room but then Brennas stopped and asked,

"Did Adelia's husband ever come here?"

"No, he never came. The house was really considered to be Adelia's. Apparently he had no liking for this part of the world and was happy for her to spend time here on her own."

Brennas had already studied Frederic's life and writing and had never come across visits to Glen Hall so that rang true. We went in search of the paintings and were taken aback when we saw what appeared to be hundreds, stacked carefully against all four walls of the dining room. Edward Wansbeck's paintings were as Romantic as Adelia's poetry, in fact, they were more than that, they were the exact depiction of the scenes from her poetry. Not only did they appear to have been lovers but they seemed to have worked together too. Brennas was beside himself.

"Imagine a book of her poetry with these paintings as illustrations!"

There were misty, melancholic water colours of Rievaulx Abbey and Fountains Abbey, dreamy landscapes of the glades and woodlands around the Hall, seascapes of the Yorkshire, Durham and Northumbrian coasts but best of all was a small portrait.

It was not a formal Victorian portrait but a picture of a lovely young woman with her long hair not tied up under a bonnet but loose and free, shifted slightly by a breeze. She was looking lovingly directly at the artist. Brennas had seen pictures of Adelia and Frederic and knew that it was her. We spent a long time looking at the paintings before going back to the library in awe at what was unravelling before us. As I worked my way through the books, I found more and more letters from Edward. I went back to all the books that I'd already catalogued, finding even more letters there carefully folded into the pages. They were all dated and, once in order, Brennas studied them. They covered a five year period of springs and autumns. Adelia was at their manor in Surrey over the Christmas period and she and Frederic travelled or visited friends in the summer so spring and autumn appeared to be the only time she could spend with her lover. Some of her writing was haunting love poetry which Brennas had presumed concerned her husband and her yearning for him during his many absences but now he knew that it was Edward, her illicit lover for whom she'd longed. Perhaps this was why her poetry was never published. If her husband had seen these verses would he have guessed that they weren't directed at him? When Brennas had studied Frederic's life and writing he'd discovered that Frederic had not been faithful to Adelia, had played about with opium and had gone off abroad without her on several occasions. Presumably, Adelia knew that she wasn't loved, that is, until she'd found solace with Edward, her poetic soul-mate.

The letters gave a whole new perspective on Adelia's life and her poetry. There were comments in the letters about trips they'd taken together. They'd been over the border to Scotland and deep into the Yorkshire Dales. In some letters Edward had made sketches of where they'd been with drawings of Rievaulx Abbey, another of Fountains Abbey, little glades and hillsides, which we now knew became the subjects of his paintings and the backcloth to Adelia's poetry.

"If only I could have the matching letters that Adelia sent to Edward." Brennas sighed. "Imagine having the full set. I wonder if Mrs. Howard knows what happened to Edward Wansbeck's belongings."

In one of the boxes there was a book on Northumbrian artists of the eighteenth and nineteenth centuries and we finally got a glimpse into Edward's life. It stated that he had never married, living the quiet life of the country bachelor. The author clearly hadn't known him. As we already knew, he hadn't become a famous painter, just as Adelia hadn't become a famous poet and yet they were both, beyond doubt, masters of their art. Perhaps they preferred not to be famous. Brennas asked Mrs. Howard about Edward Wansbeck's house and property.

"I'm afraid his house was pulled down a long time ago." She told him. "There were no heirs and it just fell into rack and ruin, long before our time."

"Do you know where his property ended up?" Brennas asked.

"No, probably auctioned, or," she hesitated, "I suppose any papers belonging to him might be in one of the county libraries or in the county archives because he was well-known locally. Would you like me to find out for you?"

"That would be wonderful if you could." Brennas replied. "You see, Mrs. Howard, we've discovered that Edward and Adelia were having an affair."

He told the warden what we'd found out. She was as excited as we were with this new information which would radically change the face of Adelia's story.

10

Our time enveloped within the life of Adelia was coming to an end. I'd catalogued the books and Brennas had obtained permission to borrow the letters. We set off for the journey back to Brennas' great aunt to take her up on her invitation to stay with her before the long haul back to London.

We arrived late morning and, after lunch, we sat in the garden, so colourful, so sweetly smelling that I felt as if I could have stayed there forever. It was not for nothing that Dottie's house was called "Eden Manor". The three of us sat in silence for a while as if the summer warmth and soft breezes had mesmerised us.

"This temperature and atmosphere reminds me very much of my time in the south of France," Great aunt Dorothy commented.

"I thought you were in Paris." Brennas said.

"Yes, I was, but we were in Antibes for most of the summers too." Dottie replied. "I haven't told many people about my time in France and I don't suppose it matters anymore. The people who would have condemned me have all gone now and these days it'll seem like nothing at all."

She then started to tell us the story, more of which I was to hear each time I visited her because this was the beginning, unknown to me at the time, of a succession of visits and a close friendship.

"In those days", she continued, "you went over to France on a steamer. I was twenty and my sister, your grandmother, Brennas, and I had come into some money from an old relative who'd died. I took my money and ran!" She laughed. "I'd always wanted to go to Paris and I reckoned that I had enough money to stay there for quite some time, perhaps even a year if I was careful. On the boat going over, I got talking to a young man, William. He was going to Paris to take charge of the English section of a bookshop in the Place de L'Opera. How strange that I had booked myself into the Grand Hotel in exactly that very same square. After the steamer docked this young man, William, and I travelled to Paris together. I loved the Grand Hotel. I was treated like a princess. I ate alone in the restaurant there that evening and I could see people wondering who this young foreign girl was who appeared to be all alone. It was wonderfully exotic!" She laughed at the memory. "The next day I went to the bookshop to see how William was settling in and he introduced me to the owner, Monsieur Lefeuvre, who then said that he really needed two people to manage the English section because he now realised that there was too much work for William to do without any help. So, he asked if I would be interested in working there and anyway my French was better than William's, or so Monsieur Lefeuvre said. So just like that, he offered me a job. I'd gone to France to wander about, not to be tied down, but, do you know, it really appealed to me. I thought of how many interesting people I might meet and how the extra money would enable me to stay on living at the Grand Hotel for a bit longer, perhaps forever!" She pulled her shawl more tightly around her and stood up.

"Shall we go inside now? It's getting a bit cold. Evenings don't retain the warmth of the day. You see, that's the difference between France and England, well, between Antibes and Durham, at any rate."

We went indoors and Dottie asked us if we would excuse her while she had a little nap. She would see us at dinner. Brennas and I went back out into the garden and he gave me a good exploration of the beautiful grounds. After the dinner provided by Dottie's housekeeper we went into the covered glass terrace that ran the length of the living room at the back of the house where we were served a glass of wine and Dottie continued the story of her French adventure.

"A very attractive gentleman, much older than me, came into the bookshop just about every day. He was treated with great respect by Monsieur Lefeuvre and he turned out to be a great Anglophile. His name was Henri and he'd talk to me about England and English writers whenever I was free. One evening he came into the Grand Hotel for dinner and was clearly astonished to see me sitting there. He asked if he could join me and said that he hoped that it didn't sound rude but he hadn't expected to see a female shop assistant having dinner at the Grand Hotel all alone. I said that I wasn't just eating there I was actually living there. I enjoyed the look on his face but then I explained my situation to him. He asked me if I would like to go to the ballet at the Palais Garnier and from then on he took me to the theatre, the opera house, out for meals, all kinds of wonderful things but always behaved as the gentleman that he was. Then when the summer came around he asked me if I was going to stay on at the bookshop or would I like to go with him to his house in Antibes for the summer. I didn't know what I was getting into but I decided to go with him. I can't even begin to describe to you how beautiful his house and garden were. He had lots of friends who called in or who stayed for dinner or drinks in the evening. We had a wonderful time, such interesting people, writers, artists, opera singers, even some politicians. He'd been a widower for many years and had never had children. He was old enough to be my father but still very handsome and with such a fine physique." She paused for a moment as if seeing him again.

"When the summer was over", she continued, "we went back to Paris but I didn't go back to the hotel or the bookshop. He invited me to stay in his apartment on the Avenue Foch. We were living there when he died, very suddenly, without warning. He hadn't been ill. He just suddenly died. I can remember clearly, weeks later, I was sitting in the drawing room so sad, so alone, wondering whether to stay in Paris or go home when his lawyer turned up and told me that Henri had left absolutely everything to me. The apartment was rented but the house in Antibes belonged to him. There was all his fine furniture, pictures, his wife's jewellery, an enormous amount of stuff to deal with. I'd kept in touch with Monsieur Lefeuvre and William from the bookshop and they and the solicitor both helped me to deal with everything. The First World War was brewing and that's when I came back here, to my roots. This house was for sale, I was rich, and that was that." She stopped and smiled. "But really, the reason I got into telling you all this is that that's where I met your Adelia, Brennas, at the house in Antibes. You were so sure that I was mistaken that I'd met her but I can remember things from decades ago far more clearly than I can remember what I did yesterday. So after you left I got out the photos that we'd had taken there and sure enough she was there. I'd written all the names on the back of the photo."

Brennas looked as if he was going to choke.

"A photo?"

She walked over to Brennas and passed it over to him, bending down to point out the various people.

"There's Henri, me, and that's Adelia there."

This wasn't just a gift from the land of Serendipity; it was a wheelbarrow full of Providence marched in by angels. No need to ask whether imps or angels were responsible for this.

"My goodness," said Brennas, "this coincidence is beyond belief. How old would she be here?"

"That photo would have been taken in about 1905 so I'd be about twenty-three and Adelia would have been about the age I am now – well into her eighties. Her husband was a lot older than her and had died long before this photo."

Of course, Brennas already knew that and pointed to a man standing next to Adelia.

"Who's that?"

"He was a painter called Edward." She hesitated for a moment. "Edward, oh dear what was his surname?" She turned the photo over and read the name on the back. "Oh yes, Wansbeck. Edward Wansbeck. He lived not far from Adelia's Northumberland house, where you've just been. All Henri's friends who visited us in Antibes were quite elderly by the time I went there. They'd all known each other since they were young."

"Edward's there too." Said Brennas as if in a trance.

She sighed. "Oh such a long time ago."

"May I borrow this photo, auntie?" Brennas asked. "And may I have it printed in the book?"

"Of course you can but do take special care of it because my dear Henri is on there. Now look at the time I really must go to bed."

"I'll just go to the car and get our things," Brennas said as he walked to the door.

When he'd gone Dottie leaned over to me and asked.

"When are you getting married, my dear?"

I wasn't expecting such a strange question.

"I don't know. I suppose I'd need a boyfriend first." I laughed and then noticing the look on Dorothy's face I realised what she meant. She meant "you" plural, as in Brennas and me.

"Oh dear, did you think that Brennas and I were, er, together? A couple? No, we're just housemates and I suppose friends now. I came with him because I have experience with archives; I was helping him with his work."

Dottie looked embarrassed and then half stood up as if she'd suddenly remembered something. She sat down again and looked confused.

"Something was on the tip of my tongue that I had to tell you but it's gone, sorry. When we were children, if we started to say something and then we forgot what it was the others would say "It must have been a lie." So it must have been a lie!"

She laughed and stood up again. Her bedroom was now on the ground floor and leaving the living room we walked along the hall to her room just as

Brennas came back into the house. As she turned the handle to go in she said that Mrs. Thompson, her housekeeper, had organised our wherewithal for the night upstairs, probably on the first floor but if not, in the attics. She wished us a good night and we thanked her, wishing her a goodnight too.

To illustrate what happened next would require words like trauma, horror and not least, acute embarrassment although we did eventually see the funny side. We went upstairs to find our bedrooms. There were four big bedrooms on the first floor and two large attic rooms on the top floor. On the first floor we found a room with the bed made up and towels arranged neatly on a towel rail.

"Ah, here's one of the rooms." Brennas said. "Let's find the other one and you can choose which one you want."

We went into the other rooms but everything there was covered in drapes.

"Oh, I see", he laughed. "They're keeping us apart."

We went up to the attic rooms. They were completely empty apart from trunks and cases with ancient labels from exotic places.

"Hell, she's only made up one bed." Brennas muttered.

Of course! Dottie had just a few minutes ago made it clear to me that she'd thought we were a couple. She had presumed that we were sleeping together. That was very modern of her I suppose but her desire to be helpful and understanding had massively backfired. I was horrified. There was no way I could sleep with him. I know it was 1970 when people were sleeping around but I felt that my relationship with him was different. I was getting to know him and appreciate him in a way different from when I'd first met him. He was becoming a good friend and I was enjoying the way our relationship was gradually developing. To suddenly become lovers was too soon. If that was ever to happen I wanted it to evolve naturally. However, it turned out that I was being presumptuous because his reaction was as horrified as mine which I must admit felt a bit insulting. That's a bit contrary, isn't it? I seemed to want it both ways.

"Look, Eve, I'm so sorry. Either Auntie didn't give Mrs. Thompson clear instructions or she's just presumed that we're a couple. What shall we do?"

"While you were out at the car your Auntie made it clear that she did think we were a couple. When I explained that we weren't she looked confused and then said there was something she needed to tell us but couldn't remember what it was. So I suppose it was this."

I was very uncomfortable and couldn't look at him.

"It's a very big bed". He said. "We could both fit in it without touching." He started laughing. "Was it King Arthur who put a sword down the middle of the bed when he first slept with Guinevere or somebody? He said that if he went beyond the sword she could kill him with it. I haven't got a sword but we could have a metaphorical one."

I was starting to find the situation slightly amusing and that made me laugh.

"I might look like a Viking but I don't actually go round raping and pillaging so let's just get a good night's sleep."

I got into the bed and lay as far as I could on the edge without actually falling out. I was so tired that despite the unease of the situation I started to doze and was in that strange semi-conscious state just before sleep when he got into the bed. He was about six foot three and his breadth was in accordance with his height so when he got in at the other side without ballast on my side of the bed, the mattress became a deep slope that rolled me suddenly into him. Because I was half asleep, in that semi-comatose state where you're half dreaming and half awake I was so shocked when I was propelled across the mattress and smashed into his chest that I screamed and in my desperation to get away, back up the hill to my own side of the bed, my legs became caught up in the sheets and instead of my feet touching the floor when I reached the edge of the bed, I was suspended head first out of the bed. Brennas couldn't help me because he was helpless with laughter for quite some time and left me there scrabbling to get back up. But he eventually leaned over, hoisted me back in and got out of the bed.

"I'll sleep downstairs on the settee." And he was gone.

Part of me was sad that he'd gone. I think my subconscious knew more about what was going on than I did. That night I dreamt or imagined that Steve, not Brennas, had put a sword down the middle of a bed. It was all too confusing.

The next morning we didn't look at each other and I felt not only embarrassed but stupid. We set off back to London, the enforced intimacy of the night before putting a strain on our relationship that had flowered after working together for three weeks. He stopped the car in a lay-by.

"Can we get this business about what happened last night out of the way? When I told aunt Dottie that we were coming to see her I made it clear who you were and why you were coming. I never implied that there was anything more to it. There was obviously a misunderstanding or possibly Aunt Dottie is becoming really dotty. Perhaps she's losing it a bit."

"I know it wasn't your fault, Brennas. It was just embarrassing, that's all."

We left it at that, gradually relaxing and talking about Glen Hall again, relishing the ridiculously wild coincidences that were happening all around us. We stopped a few times on the long route back to Kentish Town and arrived back in the early evening. There was no sign of Steve. In the three weeks we'd been away weeds had dared to spring up between the old crazy paving in our little garden and I commented that we needed to rescue it from going back to how it was.

"That lazy whatnot, Steve; he could've kept it right while we were away." Brennas said.

"But he was never interested in it, was he? He wouldn't have even noticed it needed doing."

"No, but he makes use of it now though, doesn't he?" and Brennas called Steve a few choice names.

11

In the few months that followed, Brennas visited Dottie regularly despite the long journey. He worried about her now that her memory wasn't too good and he felt that recently she'd seemed more frail. I took the opportunity of going with him. The first time we went back to visit after the farce of only one bed having been provided, I asked Brennas if he'd remembered to ask Mrs.Thompson if the sleeping arrangements could be organised differently. I felt awkward bringing this up even though we'd finally laughed it off. He replied that he'd phoned Mrs. Thompson and there was nothing to worry about. She'd been extremely embarrassed and apologetic about last time but she said that she had only done what Dottie had asked her do and it was yet another sign that Dottie was becoming forgetful.

The reason I went back was not just because it was a nice break and I had to admit to myself that I liked being with Brennas but it was also because I found Dottie fascinating and loved her stories of her time in France and then how it was when she came back to England. There was too much for her to tell in one sitting so I heard the tales in episodes each time we went. She would say,

"Now where was I up to?"

I'd always know because I was so keen to hear more. Her summers in Antibes particularly interested me. She would have that faraway look that comes over a person's face when they are deep in recollection. It was almost as if, by looking into the distance they can actually step right back into that world, join again those long-dead companions, feel the soft, warm breeze on their cheeks.

"The house was beautiful." She told me. "Almost like a small chateau. The décor was cream with gold moulding, high double doors to every room and a conservatory full of ferns, wicker chairs, rocking chairs...oh , it was so lovely." She sighed. "And the garden! My goodness, the colours and scents took your breath away. Bougainvillea, Hibiscus, all sorts of plants whose names I can't even recall. Quite often we'd have friends in for drinks or dinner or we'd have friends to stay from Paris. My favourite time though was when Henri and I would walk by the sea together, just the two of us. He said that that was his favourite time too. The evening air was still so warm that you didn't even need a shawl."

On one occasion when she was talking about the garden she told me about   her favourite part. It was a little wild area with a pond.

"The pond was rectangular, quite classical looking. There were water lilies, yellow irises and even a little waterfall. It attracted a lot of wildlife and what I loved the most were the dragonflies zigzagging over it in the late afternoon. I'd often sit there watching them with ......"

She suddenly stopped and her eyes clouded over. I thought it was the memory of sitting there with Henri that had upset her but I was to learn later that it was the memory of sitting there with someone else that had caused the pang in her heart at that moment.

She would always thank me for listening and enabling her to re-live that precious time in her life. I would always say that it was my pleasure and it genuinely was.

Brennas was quite often asked to help Mr. Thompson with some heavy work in the garden and this was usually when Dottie and I would settle down to her reminiscences. On one of our visits she took me into a huge closet off one of the bedrooms. She said that she had kept the clothes that had been especially made for her in Paris, her favourite being an almost ethereal Jacques Doucet evening dress. It fell in layers of pastel coloured gossamer that shimmered as if the summer light of Antibes had become captured in its folds. It was gorgeous, opulent, so finely made that I hardly dared touch it. We replaced it carefully but also in the closet were shawls, hats, and various other clothes from that era, some now looking bizarre but others still beautiful. Dottie insisted that I should try them on and then we played at dressing up like two children with her old clothes and hats that had been in that closet for decades. We laughed at some of the things and swooned at others. When we went downstairs Brennas was back in from the garden and he'd been listening to the hilarity. He asked us what we'd been doing and when we told him he raised his eyebrows and gave us a bemused smile.

On another of our visits she described how shortly after she'd moved into Eden Manor she'd met a woman called Eloise who became her best and most trusted friend. She wanted me to meet her but that didn't happen. She was away or she had visitors whenever we visited Dottie so I had to be satisfied with just hearing the tales of what they had done together. I did meet her much later but under very different circumstances.

"It's over fifty years since I came back to England." Dottie added. "So much has happened to me since then but those twelve years in France feel like my whole life. I think it's because life was so full and intense and, of course, I was in love. I've met a lot of men since Henri died and had offers of marriage but none of them came close to Henri. When you've had that kind of love nothing less will do. I decided I'd rather live on my own than with someone I didn't fully love."

12

When we want to change our lives, the change will come simply from the desire for it but it may not come in the form that we want or expect. Apart from our trips to Dottie's the weeks following our time in Northumberland at Adelia's house went by quickly and boringly. Brennas locked himself away to design the book on Adelia which was now going to be very different from the one that he'd envisaged when he first came upon her poetry at the manor in Surrey.

For myself, I was going through a rough patch, disliking my job and tiring of the noise and dirt of the city. I think the time in the fields of Northumberland and then Dottie's Eden in Durham had brought my dissatisfactions into the light. Should I go back up north? I had no relatives left there; they'd either died or moved away. I'd been on the late shift at the library and was feeling depressed, grumpy and hungry when I got back to the house. I went straight into the kitchen to have something to eat and found both Brennas and Steve sitting at the table. I wasn't in the mood for either of them but Brennas jumped up and said,

"Do you remember Mrs. Howard, the warden at Glen Hall? She'd said that she'd try and find out what happened to Edward Wansbeck's possessions. Well, she's located papers of his in the archives at Newcastle Central library! I've made an appointment and I'm going off there later this week."

I shook off my grumpiness so that I could genuinely congratulate him. Then he added,

"I don't really know when I'll be back. It depends on whether they let me borrow the papers or whether I'll have to work on them there."

"Will you see Dottie again?" I asked.

"Oh yes, I'll definitely call in."

"Will you give her my best wishes?" I said.

Despite remembering what her sleeping arrangements had put us through the first time I'd visited her I'd grown very fond of her over the course of out subsequent visits and I admired and enjoyed her life story. After that first visit, she and Adelia kept appearing in my dreams, with me not knowing one from the other; Dottie became Adelia and Adelia became Dottie. Glen Hall became Eden Manor; everything and everybody becoming mixed up. Every night after returning from a trip to Dottie's, those two women and those two magnificent houses swam around in my head while I slept. I had no idea why.

Brennas went off back to Northumberland. Soon the house started to feel bereft, empty, without him. I realised that he was like the soul of the house, always cheerful, optimistic, caring, unlike the caustic Steve, and me who seemed to be fed up all the time. I decided that I must sort out what I wanted to do with my life.

Although we lived in the same house I didn't see much of Steve during that week until I came home in the early evening on the following Saturday. I went into the kitchen to get my bottle of wine thinking how nice it would be to sit in the garden on such a warm summer's evening, an idea which had been in my mind when I'd first thought of renovating the garden. I remembered that I'd looked for information on how to care for a cherry tree and discovered that according to folklore, coming across a cherry tree is considered to be auspicious and fateful. As I picked up the bottle and glass I noticed that Steve was already in the garden leaning against that said fateful tree, drinking and apparently smoking. I'd never seen him smoke before. As I watched him, again the primal instinct of knowing that you're being watched hit him as it had done before when he'd caught me gazing at him. What surprised me this time was that he seemed delighted to see me and gestured to me to go out and join him. I took my bottle and glass and sat against the tree with him, noticing from the pungent smell that what he was smoking was not a cigarette which I knew he didn't smoke, but cannabis. He offered it to me and as we shared it a deep relaxation and pleasure came over me until I felt myself merge with the grass beneath me and sink into the bark of the tree at my back. We lay for a while, languid, not speaking, as the dusk gently descended and a huge full moon suddenly started to rise. It seemed so close that I felt that I could step onto it. Was it full moon madness, the cannabis, the wine? Whatever it was that was in the air, Steve suddenly leaned over, and putting his hand behind my neck pulled my face to his and kissed me. Had the Greek god really descended to my level? We went on kissing. We were young; we were beautiful; we were high; we were drunk; we were kissing. When this combination occurs one thing is inevitable. And it was. And we did.

Shards of moonbeam slanting through the branches of the auspicious cherry tree woke us in the early hours. I woke up with that feeling again of not knowing where I was which, as I'd noticed before, happens when we wake in a place that is not our own bed. Also there was something heavy lying across my stomach. I looked down and saw a man's arm. Then with amazement I remembered. I lay there stargazing through the boughs. The tree stood strong and firm in its silence. Trees never divulge who's been leaning into them; never tell what they've heard beneath them, the words, the rustling, the whispers; never tell of the hopes they feel through their bark. They absorb everything as it flows deep down into the spreading roots to the centre of the earth. Only an earthquake that tears the tree from the ground could scatter those secrets to the winds. The moon, now highly risen, watched as Steve stood up, leaned over to give me his hand and pull me to my feet. Did I feel at that moment the slight tremor of that oncoming earthquake or is that simply the trick of reminiscence?

We spent the rest of the night together in my room in my own bed. The next morning when I awoke I had no problem remembering where I was or what had happened and turned over to look at the beautiful man who had shared my bed. He was not there. The house was silent. I walked round the house but there was only the echo of my own footfall. I didn't see him for the rest of the day and I was already almost asleep in that same bed when I heard him come in late that night. As I heard him go up to his room and close his door the awful truth dawned on me. It had been just a night of pleasure for him not the beginning of a beautiful relationship which I'd so stupidly, so childishly thought at the time. I was horrified. He was stoned and drunk and I just happened to be there. That's all it was. I could have been any woman at all who just happened to be available at the time. A deep sadness and weariness overcame me.

I worked the late shift at the library during the next week and didn't see him at all until the following Saturday which was one whole week since what I'd imagined had been a magical night. He was in the kitchen and just said his usual non-committal hello. Then he came over to me.

"It's Saturday again. Do you fancy a re-play?" He said with a smile that was almost mocking.

I moved away from him.

"No, I didn't know it was just a one-night-stand." I said. "I don't do one-night-stands."

He laughed. "Yes, you do. I happen to know for definite that you do."

"But I don't because I prefer sex to be part of a relationship."

He stared at me and I saw the meaning of what I'd said dawn on him.

"So you thought we were starting a relationship?"

I couldn't bring myself to say yes, that I'd thought we were going to have a relationship when he obviously had had no such intention so I said,

"No."

"But from what you've just said, you did think that. So you'd like to be in a relationship with me would you?" He smirked and the old arrogant Steve re-appeared, so different from the marijuana-sweetened person that he'd been the week before.

"I was high and I was drunk. That's how it happened. I don't sleep around and I didn't know that you did either." I was almost shouting.

He looked at me in scornful surprise. The incredulous look that he gave me was utterly humiliating. But I was not just humiliated I was angry. But I was more angry with myself than with him. I'd been willing, hadn't I? It was totally my fault for thinking, presuming, that we were starting a relationship. He'd promised nothing but a delicious night and now I was whining about it. On top of the humiliation and anger, I now felt a fool. I left the room just as Brennas burst through the front door.

"Hey, what's up with you?" He must have read the look on my face.

To divert him I welcomed him back and asked him to tell me what had happened in Newcastle. Had it been successful? Had he found Adelia's letters amongst Edward Wansbeck's effects? He put his case down and said that what he'd found was amazing. He was walking into the kitchen as he spoke and I had no alternative but to follow him there where Steve was still sitting at the table, unconcerned, reading the paper. We sat round the table and Brennas described to us what had happened. All Adelia's letters to Edward along with more of her poems were in a carved wooden box. There were more paintings too. I was very pleased with this latest discovery in Brennas' research but I found myself busy trying to avert Steve's eyes and decided that I'd have to move house.

The next Saturday saw a race for the bathroom as the three of us tried to get ready for the wedding of Marion, my former flatmate, and Nick, Steve and Brennas' former housemate and the very reason why I came to be living there. I sat between Brennas and Steve in the church, feeling very strange and aware of Steve's closeness. After the meal and the speeches, guests stood up to dance as the band started to play and I was dumbfounded when Steve stood up and offered me his hand.

"Come on. Let's dance."

I wondered whether he was doing this deliberately to put me in a difficult position. It would have seemed unreasonable for me to refuse in front of all our friends so I reluctantly stood up. When that dance was over there was a smoochy number and I presumed we'd go back to the table but he stayed and we danced very closely.

"Are you sure you don't want a re-play, Elfie?" He whispered.

It was so tempting. We were dancing very closely, his lovely face was so close to mine. At least I would know this time that it was not the beginning of a relationship but just one of Steve's leisure pursuits. But I knew that wouldn't have suited me. I would have wanted emotional commitment in that kind of situation. I wouldn't have fared very well in a Harem. So I said no. I don't think he was used to rejection. The vain ones don't take refusal well.

Later, Brennas and I stood up to dance and Steve made fun of us, repeating a previous joke of his.

"Look everybody, it's beauty and the beast, the ogre and the elf."

Brennas repeated his previous reply to this.

"Don't call Eve a beast or an ogre."

That made everybody laugh but I gave Steve one of my looks that was the optical equivalent of a karate kick.

13

As the archives in Newcastle Library had yielded the letters that Adelia had sent to Edward, Brennas now had the full set. They shed more light on Adelia's life, her marriage to the famous poet, Frederic Stillingfleet and her poignant dreams of being with Edward Wansbeck. They showed her despair at not being able to be with him apart from their stolen times at Glen Hall. Her letters to Edward showed the source of her poetry. During the week, I read them and wondered if they reflected, too, the sadness of knowing that her husband did not, had never, loved her. Steve wasn't around much and Brennas asked me if I knew where he was. I said that I hadn't seen him for quite a while, which was true and for which I was grateful.

"He must have got back in with Cathy. This goes on all the time. It's the most on/off relationship in history." He commented as he put his food in the fridge.

"What? Steve's got a girlfriend?" I asked in amazement.

"Yeah. They've been seeing each other for ages. They split up and he goes off and has flings and then they get back together. I'm surprised he hasn't had a go at you yet."

I must have looked appalled but not for the reasons that Brennas thought.

"Well, he's a bit of a lad is our Steve. No morals. But that's what he's like, always has been, ever since I've known him."

Brennas sighed and emptied his shopping into the cupboards, fortunately not seeing the effect that this information had had on me. I asked myself again how I could have been so stupid. How could I have been so entranced, so hypnotised, by a beautiful face to the extent that I'd ignored all the evidence that he was basically not a very nice person? I had witnessed his smirking mockery, his sense of superiority, his arrogance and his vanity. Had I been willing to have a relationship with someone for the pleasure of gazing at a beautiful face disregarding the fact that underneath it all their nature didn't share the loveliness? Then I realised the truth behind the equation of beauty, the formula that decides whether you're beautiful or not. It was based on area not volume. It was a superficial measurement of façade omitting a plumbing of the depth. It was simply for artists and sculptors, not adaptable for human beings. Then another disturbing thought struck me. Had I behaved in such a way because the man involved was Steve who I was so strongly attracted to or given the same circumstances would I have acted the same way with any man, Brennas for instance, who just happened to be there in the midst of the weed and the wine? Was I at heart just the same as Steve? I had to reappraise my opinion of myself. I came out of my miserable reverie when I heard Brennas telling me that he'd called in on Dottie, his great aunt Dorothy.

"She's wondering whether to sell up. That house and garden are a bit much for her now. The Thompsons who look after her and the house are getting on and have warned her that they'd like to retire at some point but they'll wait until she can find replacements. But she doesn't really want the hassle of finding a new housekeeper and odd job man."

"Oh no, that beautiful house!" I said. "That would be such a shame. How do you feel about that? Where would she live?"

"I offered to see if I could get her new help but I think she's made her mind up. She's got a hankering to live by the sea again, North Yorkshire or Northumberland. It'll be a massive upheaval for her to move. I don't know how she'll do it unless I organise it for her."

"Would you do that?" I asked.

"Yes, but I don't think it's a good idea at her age. She's in her late eighties and she loves that house and garden. I'm sure I could get someone else to go and housekeep for her and there are local odd job men around if I can't get a couple who work together like the Thompsons. I'll think about that when I've finished writing the book. I've got everything I need now including the photos of Edward's paintings that we saw at the Hall. I thought that his painting of Adelia could go well on the front cover. What do you think?"

I was very interested in the book, having been so closely connected to the findings and we sat at the table discussing it for quite some time. At one point, I glanced up and through the window I saw the cherry tree and the garden. It would never be the same for me again. There was treachery there and the Dryads had fled.

"What's the matter?" Brennas asked and he turned round to look through the window to see where I was looking. "You look as if you've seen a ghost."

"Yes, I have."

It would have eased me to be able to tell someone how stupid I'd been and perhaps hear them say that I hadn't been stupid, that it was just one of those things in life that happens and looking back you wish you hadn't been so naïve but no harm done, just put it down to experience etc. So, I'd wanted commitment. What was wrong with that? A friend would have salved the wound but there was no-one to tell and I certainly wouldn't have told Brennas. I wasn't even sure whether Steve would tell him when they'd had a drink. I cringed at the thought.

"What did you see?" He asked.

"A memory."

"Of?"

"A mistake."

*

Life went on in that long boring straight line again that it so often does when you know that there are things that you must change but the enormous amount of energy that it would take makes it impossible for the time being. Yet again, I mused on how I was dissatisfied with my job, no longer comfortable in the house, sick of Kentish Town. Friends from my previous job lived on the other side of London and we had drifted apart. No-one in my present place of work seemed to resonate with me. It was time to go. To go from everything. I must start to look for another job. Should I even go so far as to change profession? The thought of going back up north popped up again. I was going round in circles.

Brennas came in full of his mad vivacity. "The book's going really well. Just flowing. Miraculous. And it thanks to you." He said.

I looked round to see who he was talking to and it seemed to be me.

"Come on, let's celebrate. You're down in the dumps. I'm going to buy you a drink."

We went to the local down the road and when we were settled with our drinks he asked me what the matter was. I said that I didn't know what he meant but he wouldn't have it. He said that he could see that something was wrong. Could he help?

"By the way, this'll cheer you up. When I went to see aunt Dorothy she asked after you. She said how much she liked you, how you're a good listener, a sympathetic kind of person and she was amazed at how you'd given up your time to help me at Glen Hall. And I agreed with her."

I ignored all that. "Have you played any tricks on anyone recently?" I asked.

I hadn't seen that side of him for a while. We just talked then of this and that and he didn't pry into my mood anymore. When we got back to the house Steve was in the garden leaning against the now inauspicious but definitely fateful cherry tree. The memory that this sight brought up made me recoil. He gestured for us to go out and join him.

"You thought working on the garden was a waste of time and now you're using it. We'll have to charge you." Brennas called through the open door.

I certainly wasn't going to join him in the garden and went to my room but not before I'd overheard them.

"What's up with Eve, do you know?" Brennas asked.

"She's a woman. They get crabby." Steve replied.

"So are you back with Cathy?"

"No", Steve answered. "She's gone off with some bloke from work."

Good old Cathy, whoever she was, I thought. My turn to smirk.

14

A woman's body is a calendar, the moon closely linked. Time went by and my clockwork had stopped. That night under the cherry tree started to haunt me as I realised what might be happening. My dreams became a scenario of snakes hiding behind trees as I lay against them; a wolf suddenly appearing by the birdbath; a monstrous man coming towards me, his shadow falling across me as I lay on the grass.

In those days you didn't find out if you were pregnant by sitting in the bathroom for a few minutes. No, that was too easy. You had to go to the doctor for poking and prodding and then you were referred to a hospital for confirmation which required more poking and prodding and explorations. You then waited an eternity for the verdict. So that was what I had to do. But it appeared that I had gone to the doctor too soon. I was told that I wasn't pregnant and icily given some leaflets on contraception. So I was already three months pregnant when the same doctor referred me to the Soho Hospital for Women.

On a cold, crisp autumn morning I approached the hospital and announced myself to the receptionist. She gave me a form to fill in. After waiting over an hour and a half she deigned to show me into a consulting room. The doctor was an elderly, tired looking man. He examined me and gave the verdict quite quickly that I was indeed about three months pregnant. Yes, exactly right, I thought. He looked at my notes and saw the title "Miss".

"So what do you want to do? He asked.

"I don't know." I said. "What *do* you do? I've never been pregnant before."

"I assume from your title that you're not married?" He asked wearily. "I presume you'll be wanting a termination."

I was shocked. Yes, having a child at the moment was certainly not one of the activities on my list, but an abortion? I hadn't had time to think any of this through but I knew instinctively that you don't kill your own child no matter how inconvenient they might be.

"No, I don't, I'm not going to murder my own child." I said rather pompously.

The tiredness and world-weariness on the doctor's face vanished. His face lit up.

"I so admire you for that. That's an usual decision in this day and age for someone in your situation. It'll be hard though, you know, to be an unmarried mother. Or perhaps you and the father are staying together?"

"No, that's not possible." I said.

I left in a trance. How was I going to deal with this? How and where would I live? I'd have to tell Steve. He at least had the right to know that he was going to have a child. Then I thought that perhaps I didn't need to tell him. But it takes two to create a child and he would have to take his share of the responsibility. Round and round it all went for a lifetime while I watched London pass by through the bus window. But that was not all. How would I tell Brennas? We'd become good, close friends since the days when I thought he was just a jester. As far as he knew I hardly knew Steve and whenever we were in the same room we just seemed to snipe and banter. He didn't always come out for a drink with us either so what had happened would seem confusing to Brennas to say the least. Also, perhaps Brennas wouldn't want a pregnant person in the house; a bit of a liability. He certainly wouldn't want to share the house with a squawking baby. And how would Steve react to having me and his baby in the same house? I got back to the house just as Brennas was leaving. That left Steve on his own in the kitchen. I decided to launch straight into it while I had the opportunity even though I was so nervous I felt sick.

"There's something I need to tell you."

He hardly looked up. "Yeah?"

I sat down in front of him. I knew he wouldn't like what I'd got to say so I decided to be non-confrontational and just tell him as calmly as possible.

"I know you're not going to like what I have to say but I need to tell you that I'm pregnant and it's your child."

That got his attention. "Mine? Mine?" He was practically choking. "How do I know it's mine? Why've you decided it's mine?"

"I've decided that it's yours because it *is* yours."

"But how would you know whose it is?"

I sighed. "Because before I was with you I hadn't been with anyone for over a year. I don't sleep around. Three months ago you and I had sex. I am now three months pregnant. Is that clear enough for you?"

"But how can you be pregnant? Everyone's on the pill."

"No, they're not. I'm not. Why would I be? I don't have a boyfriend and I don't sleep around, as I've told you before. What's more, I don't remember us discussing contraception at the time. You could've used something yourself. You initiated it."

"Oh yes, so it's all my fault."

"No it isn't. That's not what I'm saying. It's a joint responsibility."

"So you had sex knowing you weren't on the pill?"

"So you had sex without asking me if I was on the pill?"

We were getting nowhere.

"So I suppose you want the money."

"What money?"

"For the abortion."

"I'm not having an abortion."

"What? Are you mad?"

His thinking was a bit quick. Had he been here before?

"I don't want anything from you. I just thought that you had the right to know that you're going to have a child. If you want to share the cost of its upkeep that would be good."

"No, I won't, because I think you should just get rid of it. Why should I pay for it if I don't want it?"

I just left the room. There was nothing more to be said. I would have to continue working out how I was going to deal with this. The doctor was right though – it was still difficult to have an illegitimate child. I'd have to face disdain and disapproval, perhaps give up the chance of ever getting married, even face discrimination in anything I wanted to do in the future. Perhaps it was just a pipe dream to have this child but the magic had started to work. I was getting to know the child; to talk to it; to think of it growing up.

Next morning, Brennas bounced in and asked me if I'd like another trip up to aunt Dottie's at the weekend. Could I take next Friday and Monday off so we could spend a bit more time there. He'd arranged to go up to see her and he told me that she'd particularly asked if I would be going again too. The thought of getting away for a bit appealed to me and I agreed to ask for the time off. When Brennas had gone upstairs Steve looked up and said,

"You go up north a lot with Brennas, don't you? You were definitely up there with him about three months ago."

I suddenly remembered the sleeping arrangements that Dottie had provided for us when we'd first stayed with her and wondered if Brennas had told Steve. Steve might not have believed that Brennas had slept on the sofa and that we'd sorted out the mix up on our later visits.

"What are you insinuating?" I asked.

"Just reminding you." He said coolly.

"There's nothing to remind me about. Everything I've said to you is true so please just face it and stop making accusations."

I left the room but I was trembling with anger, frustration and fear as to what the future might hold. I'd known that Steve would not like the news but I hadn't thought that he might just deny it or free himself from all responsibility for it. Would it matter that my child wouldn't know their father? *I* knew who he was so I could describe him to the child. But how would I explain that their father didn't want them, had even wanted them to be exterminated? Just yet another problem.

15

Great aunt Dorothy was as pleased to see me as she had been on all my previous visits. We had lively chats and a delicious lunch after which Dottie excused herself to go for her post prandial nap, as she called it.

Brennas and I sat in the relaxing living room but it was anything but relaxing for me. I decided that this was my chance, away from the house and Steve, to tell him that I was pregnant. I wanted him to hear it from me, not in any other way. I needed to know as soon as possible if he didn't want me in the house anymore, for whatever reason.

"Brennas, I've got something that I need to tell you. It's very important. It's ......"

I wanted to say something like - it's something very strange, unusual, tragic, just to prepare him but I couldn't think of the right word.

"Have you got another job at last? You're not moving out are you?" He asked, looking concerned.

"I'm having a baby." No point beating about the bush.

He looked utterly bewildered for a few moments as if I'd spoken in some ancient language that he'd never heard before. But then it wasn't only bewilderment; I could see disappointment. Disappointment in me not being the person he thought I was. It was as if there'd been a pedestal that I hadn't been aware of and I'd fallen off it.

"But, I didn't even know you had a boyfriend." He finally said.

"I haven't."

"Then, how … I don't understand. I didn't think you were like that." He blurted out.

"I'm not *like that.* I don't sleep around, I never have done. It was a massive mistake, an unexpected one-night-stand. I was high and drunk."

"Did this person get you drunk?"

"It was my own bottle of wine. I've got no excuse."

"Do I know him?"

I couldn't reply. I felt tears coming into my eyes.

"Oh, no. It was Steve wasn't it? Bloody typical. The bastard. I'll kill him. I warned you once what he was like."

"It was already too late by then."

"Have you told him?"

"Yes."

"I bet he was delighted." He responded sarcastically. "I suppose he expected you to have an abortion and you've refused."

How well he knew us both.

"That's right. I know you won't want all the chaos of pregnancy and a baby in the house so I'll move out."

"Where will you go?"

"I don't know yet." The tears were streaming now.

"You don't have to move out." He said it so softly I hardly heard him. "Don't go. We'll manage. If anyone should leave it's Steve."

I heard Dottie moving about and quickly dried the tears. She came back into the room looking so elegant. Her hair was smoothed into a French pleat showing spectacular gold and ruby earrings which reached halfway to her shoulders. She was wearing a red and green shawl which she declared was sixty years old having been bought for her in a Moroccan souk by the beloved Henri on one of their many trips there. She was in her eighties but looked timeless and beautiful. I admired her earrings and she told us the story of how Henri had had them made especially for her at his jewellers on the Rue de Rivoli. Listening to her stories was balm to my agitated soul and by bed-time I had calmed down.

It was nearly midnight when we parted for bed. Mrs. Thompson had prepared two bedrooms again.

We didn't ever find out if Mrs. Thompson had told Dottie about the mistake with the bed on our first visit but we thought that she probably hadn't as Dottie would have been mortified. As we parted, Brennas said that we must talk about "the other thing" when we got back home. I was so fortunate that he'd become my best friend. I'd thought that we were possibly becoming more than just friends but I'd ruined that possibility now. As I lay down in the softest bed I'd ever slept in I went over in my mind the steps that had led me to this moment and this condition. It started at great uncle Robert's funeral and cousin Pete inviting Brennas to attend. I now presumed that the series of coincidences that had emanated from that were wrought by the imps not the angels. But who could know at this point? We weren't there yet; we weren't at the end and able to look back. Only later when you stand back and see the whole picture can you decide whether it was Providence or the other, for which I, as yet, still didn't have a name.

We'd gone to Dottie's by train. On the way back to London Brennas brought up "the other thing" and he was working out how I would manage. I was wondering why he was taking this upon himself when it had nothing to do with him. It was as if he was taking on the role of the parent or guardian of a young naïve girl who'd been abused. I found it annoying but as he was the only person I'd talked to about it so far I suppose I was grateful too. He was muttering again about breaking Steve's neck so I had to remind him that I had

had some choice in the matter. He then said something that startled me.

"Well, shall we put it that he took advantage of you because he must have noticed how infatuated you were with him."

Humiliation seemed to be becoming part of my life.

"Is that what he said?" I asked.

"He didn't need to. It was obvious the way you ogled him every time he was in the room and you never had a normal conversation with him."

I hadn't realised that my gaping at Steve had been noticed. Brennas had never said anything nasty to me before and it hurt. I felt like a foolish young teenager who'd had a crush on a boy and was being reproved for it. I picked up the newspaper that I'd bought at the station and opened it up so that it completely hid my shamed face. He gently pulled the paper down, said sorry, and opened his book.

When we got back to the house Steve was in the kitchen so I went straight up to my room. I heard the rumble of a long conversation and then shouting. Presumably Steve was being ticked off for debasing a maiden who had no freewill. Perhaps he was even having his neck broken which was what Brennas had said he wanted to do.

Later, I went out into the garden and lay against the once magical cherry tree. I'd thought that I'd never be able to go out there again but I'd reclaimed it. I closed my eyes and sank into the grass until a shadow fell across me, just as it had done in a dream. I was not pleased to see that it was Steve who had come out to join me, asking if we could talk. I decided that Brennas had told him to do this and that it had not come from Steve himself so it was therefore worthless. He sat down.

"Apparently I reacted badly when you gave me the news." He said. "But it was such a shock, you know. It seemed like ages ago and it really took me by surprise. I'm not going back on what I said though. I don't want a baby. I'm right at the beginning of my career, babies just aren't part of my plan at the moment. There are lots of things I want to do. It's not what I want at this point in my life."

"It's not part of my plan either." I responded. "But we created it so we both have to take responsibility."

"Listen to yourself." He said. "You're so self-righteous."

I didn't know what to say. There was nothing to say in answer to that. So I said nothing. We were both sitting where we'd been sitting on that portentous night and I remembered how he'd drawn me to him for that first kiss. I turned and looked at him, able to appreciate how it had happened. Michelangelo's formula was still working its magic even though I knew now that it was only true for facades, only superficial. The cherry tree started digging into my back. It had never done that before. I stood up and went back into the house.

16

The months rolled by and the baby was making its presence visible. I kept out of Steve's way and didn't see him at all. Brennas was busy with his book and as my social life up to that point had revolved round him, his friends and my old flat mate, Marion, I was left very much to my own devices. One Saturday I was in the kitchen when Brennas came in looking serious.

"I've got something to tell you. It's something you need to know." He said as he sat down across the table from me.

I looked up wondering what else could possibly be going to happen. Was he going to tell me that he was giving the house up and that I'd have to move? Had he decided that, after all, a baby in the house would be too disruptive? Then he said,

"It's that he's gone. Steve. He's gone."

"Gone?" I asked. "What do you mean – gone?"

"Before you and Steve er, you know, "got together" he'd applied for a job in Australia. And just before you gave him the news, he'd found out that he'd been offered the job. That's another reason why he reacted so badly to the news, apart from him just being a selfish bastard anyway. So he accepted it and he's gone now, to Australia."

It all seemed surreal. I suppose I'd thought that as time went by and the child grew up he might take an interest but I don't know why I'd thought that because it was highly unlikely.

"The last time we spoke he didn't tell me any of that. He didn't even say goodbye."

"Well, he wouldn't, would he?" Brennas responded.

This news deflated me more than I dared show. I knew there was no future with Steve and I didn't even like him as a person but not to say goodbye? Did he have no desire whatsoever to know his own child? He's inhuman.

"So are you going to get another house-mate or move or what?" I was scared, dreading the answer. I knew Brennas very well by now so I don't know why I mistrusted what he might do.

"No, I'm not going to get anyone else in." Was all he said.

"But what about the rent? I won't be able to pay half his share of the rent. I can't afford it."

"I don't need his share of the rent. I inherited everything from my grandparents. I don't even need to work. That's why I don't mind earning a pittance from these books I write because it means I can just indulge my passion for these topics that seem to only interest schools and academics."

I remembered Steve saying that Brennas was "filthy rich" and making fun of his love for poetry. He stood up and got some beer out of the fridge.

He looked at me and said "You've never mentioned your parents in all the time I've known you. Are they still around?"

"They're divorced. My father went off abroad and never kept in touch. Oh, that's odd, isn't it? His grandchild will be in exactly the same situation. My mother remarried but we'd never got on very well so it's just down to birthday and Christmas cards now."

"Are you going to tell her about her grandchild? That might make things better between you." He said.

"That's exactly what would make things worse." I said with a grim laugh. "She's one of those people who's always bothered about what other people will think. She'd have hysterics if she knew I was having a baby without being married and she'd be of no help whatsoever. When someone we knew, who wasn't married, got pregnant she called her shop-soiled goods, a slut, no better than a prostitute. So, no, I won't be telling her; I'm not going to put myself through that. It'd be a lifetime of recrimination."

Brennas' great aunt Dottie had stopped saying that she wanted to move and Brennas had been looking for replacements for the Thompsons. Dottie and I had forged a lovely relationship during my many visits. I was truly fond of her and she was always very affectionate towards me. Her forgetfulness was apparent as it became clear that she was still under the impression that Brennas and I were a couple. Each time she implied it we put her right but the information didn't seem to stick. I knew that if I went to see her now that the baby was showing she would be convinced that she was about to become a great-great aunt. Also, the thought of the long journey didn't appeal to me so I reluctantly didn't go the next time he travelled up to see her.

"She was disappointed that you didn't go with me." He said when he got back. "She's taken a liking to you. Can't imagine why."

He laughed at his own joke and passed over a little package.

"She wants you to have these."

I was stunned. They were the spectacular gold and ruby earrings that I'd admired once when we were there.

"Wow, that's amazing. I can't believe it. They're so beautiful!" I said as I went to the mirror to try them on. "I must write and thank her."

I wondered whether she'd given them to me because she thought that I was Brennas' girlfriend or because she really did like me. It didn't really matter.

So life plodded on by as I got bigger and bigger. There were odd looks from people at work, some of the older ones no doubt now thinking of me as the fallen woman, as Dottie had said that she would have been so named if she hadn't returned to England with a wedding ring and lots of money. It was strange how the stain of unmarried pregnancy was still so ingrained in people's minds despite the imagined liberation of the nineteen-sixties. I tolerated the looks and whispered asides because this was what my life would be like from now on. I kept telling myself that it was no-one else's business but it was hard nonetheless. Most of the people at work were either older than me or they were married so there'd never been any social life connected with work. In fact, if I hadn't inherited Brennas' friends and retained Marion's friendship, I don't know what I would have done in the evenings or weekends. His friends didn't ask about the baby, not to me anyway. I don't know whether he'd told them or whether they'd just presumed it was his.

One evening while I was eating my dinner in the kitchen, the phone rang just as Brennas was bounding down the stairs. He joined me in the kitchen.

"That was Mrs. Thompson. She's saying Dottie's forgetfulness is getting quite bad, to the extent that it could be dangerous if she's in the house on her own. They're asking if they should move into the house. It's no good, I'll have to go back up and see if I can sort something out."

The Thompsons lived in a cottage that Dottie owned. It was on the edge of the garden and the arrangement had suited them well over the years.

122

Brennas still hadn't finished writing and arranging his book on Adelia because of the frequent trips up north and he was becoming frustrated.

"I don't know how long I'll be away. Why don't you come too?" He asked. "Have a break."

But I couldn't let Dottie see me pregnant and I couldn't have coped with the long journey. I was still working and I didn't want to do anything to jeopardise my job. I'd need it more than ever when my maternity leave finished which in those days wasn't for very long. That was a vain hope as it turned out.

I was called into the Chief Librarian's office where it was explained to me that they needed to make some redundancies and as I was about to have some considerable time away from work then I was one whom they much regretted they would have to let go. I knew that he was lying. He knew that he was lying. He should have said what was really on his mind which was that someone with a baby is a liability. Babies are sometimes ill; babies need a lot of looking after. This person doesn't even have a husband so she'll have to do it all herself. She'll take a lot of time off. They could think like that in those days and act like that. No appeal, they could do what they wanted. So, at the end of the month there'd be no job, no money.

I didn't waste any time. I went to the Social Security Office. More humiliation awaited me as I queued with all the other unfortunates, or in my case, the stupid people. I had a degree, I had a postgraduate diploma,

I'd had a professional position and now? I crawled along in the filthy office to beg money from the government because one magical summer's evening Michelangelo's David had stepped off his plinth and offered himself to me. This was the beginning of the self-loathing that was to fester while I worked my notice and then went back to the empty house every evening. The saying that you make your own bed so you'll have to lie in it was ironically appropriate. I knew I had to stop this downward spiral. I'd realised what I'd taken on and it had frightened me.

It was a relief when Brennas returned and his vibrant energy filled the house once more. He had managed to hire a retired nurse who would live in with Dottie and the Thompsons could stay in their cottage. There was still the problem of their eventual retirement but for the time being all was well. I didn't tell Brennas about losing my job and I eventually got the date for my interview with Social Security.

I'd already filled in the endless forms and this was the final hurdle. What helped me to pull away from my black mood was that the person I saw for the interview turned out to be a friendly, polite young woman of about my own age who dealt with everything as if it was all perfectly normal; no tutting; no slapped wrist, no haughty demeanour. I realised that this was all in a day's work for her as I was certainly not the first woman to come into her office with this kind of problem. She was also efficient and I left the office with the knowledge that my rent would be paid and that I would have just about enough to live on each week. How lucky I am, I thought, living in a civilised country which remains civilised even when there are so many uncivilised, undeserving people living in it, like me, for example. That was the last time I took a swipe at myself and I settled down to make the plans for the arrival of the little being who was growing rapidly and who I'd started having conversations with, getting to know him or her very well as he or she danced the night away.

Christmas was approaching. Marion and Nick invited Brennas and me to spend Christmas Day with them in their new house, this being their first Christmas as a married couple. Later in the day, more friends arrived and I was surprised to find myself enjoying it all. I then thought of how different next Christmas would be. The child would be eight months old by then, old enough to be transfixed by the Christmas tree lights, delighted by a new teddy bear and the centre of my attention.

When we got back home, Brennas brought out a parcel that he said aunt Dottie had asked him to give to me at Christmas. He warned me that she'd said that it wasn't new, in fact it must be about sixty years old. Inside the parcel was a slim cardboard box. Folded into sheets of smooth white tissue paper was a dressing gown or house-coat as it may have been called in those days, of thick black satin with lavish, overblown pink roses flowing diagonally across it. There was a label inside stating "Maison Paquin. Paris." I remembered how Dottie and I had played with her clothes that

Saturday afternoon a few months ago; how we'd giggled and laughed. The garment was so luxurious, so beautiful, that not for the first time recently, I couldn't speak.

He said that she was sorry that I didn't visit anymore so he'd decided to tell her why I wasn't going and what had happened. He apologised to me for telling her without my permission but he said that it was necessary because she seemed upset that I'd stopped going. She'd been wondering why it could be. Had Brennas and I fallen out?

"I also told her that the father of your child had abandoned you. I said that because it's true. Anyway, the point is that she said that if you could manage the journey she'd still love to see you again."

He was going up there regularly now and I decided to go with him the next time he went. I also wrote to her, thanking her for the gift and repeating what Brennas had already told her about the baby, also telling her how much I was looking forward to seeing her again. I received a beautifully written letter back from her and our lovely relationship was re-established as several letters and gifts floated between Eden Manor and dusty old Kentish Town. According to what happened next I believed that the letters had the marks of orchestration on them. I was so grateful that we had been in touch so recently.

17

1971

My next visit to her house was very different from the one that I'd expected. I was very pleased that we'd been in touch so recently because I hadn't known that the letters would be the last time we would send our thoughts to each other, on this plane at least. Mrs. Thompson had called late one night to tell Brennas that his lovely great aunt Dorothy, dear Dottie, had had a stroke. She had died, never regaining consciousness. It had been out of the blue, quick, no suffering.

We were heartbroken, inconsolable. Nothing could relieve us of the loss of Dottie from our lives. Brennas had to go straight up to her house because as he was the next-of-kin he had to organise the arrangements. He asked me to go with him and I was painfully aware that I'd said to him that the next time he went to see her I would go with him. You never know when something is the last time that you'll do it or the last time that you'll see someone. I pondered on how much nicer we would be to everyone if we imagined that it was the last time we would see them. I suppose the only time we know for sure that we'll never speak to someone again is the moment before their execution. But there's always the chance of a pardon right up to the last minute so even in that extreme case we never really know. The beautiful house had taken on a melancholic air. I did what I could in the house while Brennas was out arranging the funeral, seeing solicitors; all the things that have to be done at a time in your life when all you want to do is to sit quietly and nurse your grief.

The funeral was to be at the ancient Norman church that stood on a hill close to the house. It was difficult to imagine that the sprightly, endlessly fascinating Dottie was not with us anymore. How could her animation just disappear like that? The church was pleasingly simple with plain white walls and little decoration. The stained glass window behind the altar was of Jesus the loving shepherd, not Jesus, the persecuted prisoner. The stained glass windows along the side walls were equally benign, no tortures or martyrdoms to dismay you as you attempted to pray. I told Brennas that I would go to the church early so that I could sit at the back. He was adamant that I should sit with him in the front pew which was reserved for family only and so would I keep him company? Did I want him to sit on his own? He also asked the Thompsons and Dottie's nurse to join us.

It was a sharp, frosty morning but with a clear blue sky. The tall, bare trees that lined the drive up to the entrance to the church seemed to be standing to attention as we walked slowly along. The church was full when we arrived. There were even people overflowing into the graveyard. Everyone watched as we walked to the front. Dottie had lived there for over fifty years and was well known and liked in the area. We weren't surprised to see so many people. They also knew Brennas, at least by sight and I received odd looks as I walked in beside him. Funerals always pull you out from the very centre of your being. We sometimes drift off into selfish thoughts of our own quietus, the way, the when, the how. I remembered how strange it was that I'd first met Brennas at my own great uncle's funeral and now here I was accompanying him to his great aunt's funeral after all this time and after all the strange tides that had ebbed and flowed since meeting him. We'd become such close friends despite our unfortunate start.

After the service, we stood outside so that Brennas could thank everyone for coming and invite them to the reception which was to be in the quaint parish hall next door. As the congregation came out of the church they shook Brennas' hand, mourning his loss on the one hand and congratulating him on the baby on the other.

"One departs and one arrives." They'd say.

Brennas quickly explained that I was his colleague from London and a friend of Dottie's. He muttered that it would be easier just to accept their congratulations because it was highly unlikely that we'd ever see any of them again. How wrong that comment turned out to be. As we walked over to the old church hall Brennas whispered to me that if I saw anyone freeloading at the buffet I must interrogate them but not to forget that they might be the chaplain. I feigned annoyance at the reference to how I'd treated him at my great uncle Robert's funeral but we chuckled at the memory as we walked into the hall. I was hoping to keep a low profile but there was too much interest in this pregnant stranger who appeared to be with Dottie's great nephew. He had to keep hauling me out to introduce me to her old neighbours and friends, explaining that when I'd been working in the area I'd got to know Aunt Dorothy and we'd become friends. I'd just managed to sit back down when a lady, possibly as old as Dottie and as fashionable and attractive as she had been, approached me.

"I think you must be Eve?"

I said that I was and she asked if she could sit and talk to me for a while.

"I'm Eloise, one of Dottie's oldest friends."

"Oh yes, she mentioned you a lot." I said, brightening up at the thought of meeting her at last. Dottie had spoken of her as one of the first people she had befriended when she came back to England and they had stayed good friends over all the decades that had followed.

"She was very taken with you, Eve. She said that you reminded her of herself when she was your age. There was something in your attitude, your spirit, that resonated with her."

"I felt that link." I responded. "We developed a kind of bond."

"I remember clearly the first time she told me her story." Eloise continued. "I hadn't known her long but we'd connected immediately just as you and she did. I often thought how brave she was, coming back here, buying the house while all the time grief-stricken by the loss of her husband and son."

"Son?" I gasped.

"Oh, my goodness, You didn't know? That's typical of Dottie. I'm sure that when she was told that you were pregnant she decided not to tell you in case it upset you. You don't tell a pregnant person about a baby dying but now I've done it. I'm so sorry."

She looked genuinely distressed but I was desperate to know this part of Dottie's life that she hadn't yet told me.

"Please tell me, Eloise. It won't upset me. This is part of Dottie's life that I know nothing about. It would be such a shame if I didn't know her whole story especially if she'd had a baby."

"If you're sure, then I will tell you so that you can fully appreciate Dottie's life. She had a wonderful relationship with Henri. Their life sounded like a fairy tale. Then she discovered that she was pregnant. She and Henri had never married and she was wasn't sure how he'd take the news. It turned out that he was overjoyed, more than that, he was ecstatic. He'd been going to suggest that they marry but he'd been bothered that the age difference might deter her and he hadn't wanted to spoil their time together. He'd admitted that he was worried that she might meet a man more her own age and eventually leave him. Marriage would have tied her to an old man. But she told me that nothing would have deterred her from marrying that lovely man and so that's what they did, just a quiet, simple ceremony. The baby was a boy and they called him Desiré, French for "the desired one" because that's what he was. When he was only about a year old he died. It was one of those infant deaths where there doesn't seem to be any cause. They thought it must have been their fault in some way and suffered terribly. It wasn't long after that that Henri suffered his fatal heart attack. When she came back from France she was mourning for both her son and her husband."

I remembered Dottie telling me that she'd watched dragonflies by her pond in Antibes and then she'd suddenly stopped when she was about to say who she'd been watching them with. I imagined her now sitting there with her precious son, who'd been her little companion for only one year. I had tears in my eyes by now and Eloise worried that she had indeed upset me. I said no, in fact I was grateful to her for telling me, for finishing Dottie's story for her.

"She and I met quite by chance at a mutual friend's house." She continued. "It was strange. We didn't have to go through all the social niceties, it was as if we already knew each other. I can't believe she's not here anymore."

By this time we were both crying. When the reception was over we said our goodbyes and Brennas and I went over to Eden Manor to stay the night but without the loving company of Dottie as I will always think of her, not as great aunt Dorothy.

The next day I had to get back to London as I was still working my notice and I didn't want to give them an excuse not to pay me my last full month's salary. I left Brennas at the house to continue with the tiring aftermath demanded by law and by society when someone has departed and I trekked back on the long journey.

I still hadn't told Brennas that I'd lost my job. My last day at the library finally arrived and I was very surprised to see that they'd bought me a present. Hypocrisy is a strange thing. I now had hours of time to fill. I meandered around London, going to the places that I'd passed every day but had never had time, energy or perhaps in some cases, the inclination to visit. Museums, art galleries, the homes of historic figures saw me wend my way through their fascinations. I'd wander across Hampstead Heath; I'd float along Parliament Hill and down into the Vale of Health. The roses in Queen Mary's garden in Regent's Park watched me sitting there for many an hour. St. James' Park, Green Park, in fact all the parks, any park I could find would be worn down by my weary feet. I read novels, newspapers, magazines, books on how to deal with babies, books on how to be a good parent. If anything had been written, I read it.

On some evenings Marion would visit if she could or I'd go to a club with the little gang of friends who I'd been introduced to by Brennas on that day of destiny when we'd first met. I discovered the pleasures of watching a film at a weekday matinee when children and teenagers were at school and there was no-one to play the fool or crackle sweet papers. So I suppose all in all I was having quite a nice time. It was like a holiday, especially if I could forget about the future for two seconds.

Brennas came back to Kentish Town while Dottie's solicitor worked on the legalities. He was hoping to catch up with his work that had been so frequently interrupted during the past few months. I was sitting in the garden when he returned that afternoon so he was surprised to see me.

"Are you ok? Oh, I suppose you're on the late shift, are you?" He asked.

"I'm a lady of leisure now."I responded.

"Surely it's too early for maternity leave?"

I had to tell him what had happened and I was pleased to see that it made him furious.

"Of all the times to take someone's livelihood away! They're inhuman." He flared.

I explained that I could still pay the rent and pay my way and not to worry about that. He was furious again that I'd had to go to Social Security.

"I've told you before that I have more money than I'll ever need. I wouldn't have minded if you had no money. You could still have gone on living here."

"But why, Brennas? We're not related. You're not responsible for me. I couldn't live here without paying rent."

"You're my muse." He said. "You understand my work and I can talk to you about it and that's worth a lot to me. Most people think I'm wasting my time. What was it Steve said? I spend my time fannying around with dead poets. Anyway, I don't want to live on my own and it's a hassle to get a lodger, especially someone you don't know. Better the devil you know...." He said with that grinning challenging look.

We'd gone to sit in the garden and I felt relief that I could go on living there and for the time being at least everything was manageable. What it would be like after the baby was born I had no idea. I didn't dare bring it up. Brennas had his own life to lead, he was a free agent. He'd almost finished the book on Adelia and I didn't know what he'd do next or where it would take him. I realised that I mustn't start to rely on him. I must make a plan. I leaned against the cherry tree and let all the thoughts drift away so that just for those few moments I could have no fears for the future because this moment now was perfect. The Dryads were back. I heard their whispers drifting on the air.

18

Time went by as it tends to do, ruthless and impatient. Brennas had practically finished his book on Adelia Stillingfleet which I was proofreading for him step by step, mentally back at Glen Hall. Eventually Dottie's solicitor got in touch with Brennas asking him to go to their office to sign papers as he was the executor. I was only a short time off giving birth and couldn't go back to see Eden Manor for one last time. He promised to be back soon and had apparently informed Marion and Nick and the gang that I would be on my own. It was strange but delightful that he was taking care of me when none of my problems were of his making and I remember how awful and ashamed I'd felt when he'd said "I didn't think you were like that" when I told him what had happened. I remembered the look of disappointment in his eyes when he'd realised that I was just like all the other girls who had fallen for Steve. He must have previously thought I was different in some way. I was sad about that.

Human beings have free will but when they use it in a selfish way we call it being wilful. This quality of being "full of will" can start at a very early age, in fact, when the creature is still in the womb and not even an independent person. I say this because my child, deliberately, or so I fancifully thought at the time, decided to be born while I was on my own at two o'clock in the morning. Brennas was still away and I certainly wouldn't phone friends in the early hours so I picked up my case that was already packed and took myself off to the hospital. I remembered to scrawl a quick note to Brennas telling him where I was.

I wasn't made to feel very welcome at the hospital; I was a bit of a nuisance turning up at that time and alone. You'd have thought that I'd done it on purpose just to annoy them. They put me in admissions and forgot about me. When the day staff came on they didn't seem to know much about me and as the labour was well under way by then I wasn't in the mood for a chat. I will draw a veil over the following hours of pain and the failings of a large understaffed hospital because the result was a perfect baby boy who already had black hair and huge eyes. He had a round head, a round body, round hands, round feet; he was a podgy set of conjoined circles.

I spent that night in a room on my own and was able to sleep deeply. As I awoke in the morning, coming to, I remembered that it was all over and that I had a perfectly beautiful baby boy who would be mine forever. But that thought flooded me with an inundation of emotion which made me desperate to protect him. When he was grown up, out in the world, anything could happen to him; he could be hurt; he could suffer; he could be out in that world alone; as a young man he would be called upon to go to war, to fight, to be killed. I wondered how I could save him and the answer came – love. I understood then the strength of love. It was a protective coating around those you loved, a forcefield.

But then another dreadful thought entered this agitated mess that my mind had become. Babies of unmarried mothers were taken away for adoption, often without the mother knowing. A young nurse came in, saying she was taking the baby away for a bath. I became desperate, almost hysterical, trying to get out of the bed and forbidding her to take him. She looked frightened and ran from the room, returning moments later with the Sister. The Sister was an older, kindly woman who asked me calmly why I didn't want the baby to be bathed. I explained that it wasn't the bath I was worried about, it was the abduction of my baby. I told her my horrific thoughts.

"That could only happen in one of those despicable homes for unmarried mothers, my dear. But this is an NHS hospital. It would be against the law for us to allow a baby to be removed. He's safer here than anywhere else in the whole world."

She moved the hair out of my eyes.

"Do you have a brush, dear? Whenever my own hair's tangled I can never think straight. Let me brush your hair for you."

And so she did while I cried for the inexistent death in an inexistent war of my existent son. I cried for the women whose babies had been torn away from them in the name of propriety. I cried for Dottie and her Desiré.

"After we've given birth, our hormones are all over the place but they do settle down." The Sister told me.

She had calmed me down in such a sweet, simple way. She was one of the nice ones.

Later on that day I was wheeled into a ward where there were three beds facing me and three beds on my side of the room, including mine. There was a visiting hour in the afternoon but no-one knew I was there so of course I had no visitors. I saw looks coming my way from the other women and their visitors. Then it turned out that in the evenings the rule was that only husbands could visit so even if my friends had known I was there I still wouldn't have had a visitor. I noticed the women in the beds opposite me saying something to their husbands who would then turn round and sneak a look at me. Someone had once said to me that I would never need to learn Martial Arts because I could knock someone down with just a look so I used this ability to full effect.

The next day, those who were able to potter about were having a gossip together with the occasional look coming my way. They didn't speak to me. All these dutifully married women knew what sort of person I was. In those days the stay in hospital after a birth was much longer than it is now so I had lot of disapproval to work through.

On the third afternoon as I lay propped up in bed listening to the babble of visitors I caught sight of a spider's web across the outside of the window. It was acting like a lace curtain and through its latticework I could see a church spire in the distance against a blue sky. It was April, the golden month, the month of forsythia, daffodils, celandine. I longed to be out on the heath away from this toxicity.

Suddenly, a shape blocked out the light from the corridor and there, filling the doorway, was Brennas' massive frame. He was looking for me and when he caught sight of me he strode confidently across the room looking truly like his nickname, the Viking, with his long auburn hair, matching beard and forbidding size. I chuckled to myself as I thought how magnificent he looked. Never had I been so pleased to see him. As he approached my bed a frisson of interest quivered through the harpies in the ward. He took my hand, kissed it and seated himself by the bed. He'd only just returned from Durham, found my note and was in time for afternoon visiting. We talked for a while about the baby and the birth and he asked if Marion and Nick and been in. I told him that no-one knew I was there and so I'd had no visitors.

"That's why you're the centre of attention." I told him. "You're the first visitor I've had and – you're a man."

We laughed. I whispered to him about how the other women were treating me. He thought for a while and then said that he'd thought of something that would solve it. Oh no, I thought, not one of Brennas' tricks. He was obviously thinking of a way of bringing them down. It would make matters even worse. But he said no, it would work. At the end of visiting time he was walking away but half way down the ward he stopped and called back to me.

"Chin up! Only a few more days and he'll be home on leave!"

Another alert rustle of interest swished through the coven.

Later, as we moved about the ward, the chief witch whom I'd mentally christened Hecate approached me and said,

"Your visitor mentioned leave. Is your husband in the Forces?"

I hoped they didn't ask me which regiment he was in or where he was based. I knew nothing about the army. Or could he be in the Navy or even the RAF? I was cursing Brennas. I hadn't had time to plan my imaginary husband's career. Then, sure enough, she asked me where he was stationed. A brainwave dawned on me.

"He's in the Special Forces. I never know where he is. They're not allowed to say. His leave was planned around the due date but the baby came a week early."

"Oh you poor soul", Hecate exclaimed, "not even knowing where your husband is and the baby coming early. That's so hard. When you didn't have any visitors and you don't wear a wedding ring we thought .. you know ...."

I maintained my steady gaze. I didn't help her out.

"You thought?"

"Well, you know, we thought you weren't married, you know, one of those unmarried mothers."

"And would that have made a difference?" I asked, smiling, maintaining eye contact.

I could swear that a look of shame spread across her face but I went back to my bed.

That evening the husbands trooped in probably straight from work in crumpled suits, looking weary and pale. There were muffled whispers and sidelong glances at me again. When the husbands left, this time they looked at me, smiled and nodded a good-night. I had gone from slag to wife of a hero within minutes. When Brennas played his dramas he certainly knew his audience.

The news of the birth spread amongst my friends and I was deluged with flowers. Marion and Nick managed half an hour before the end of afternoon visiting, having left work early to see me. A member of the old gang who was a musician worked in the evenings so he came by one afternoon causing as big a stir as Brennas had. He was the image of Jimi Hendrix and had his guitar with him. I swear Brennas had put him up to it.

I was so besotted with my lovely baby that the world had become a magical place. The day was coming when I'd be able to leave the hospital and Brennas was visiting again, sitting by the bed.

"Have you thought of a name for His Majesty yet?" He asked.

"Yes." I replied. "I'm going to call him Desiré, the desired one, because that's what he is."

He looked startled.

"You know? How on earth do you know? This couldn't possibly be a weird coincidence because if it is, it's positively supernatural. Auntie Dot said she'd decided not to tell you about her son in case it upset you."

"No, it's not one of those coincidences that seem to be so prevalent in my life." I replied.

I told him about the conversation that I'd had with Eloise. She hadn't known that I didn't know about Dottie's son when she mentioned it and so we mustn't blame her. Brennas was quiet for a moment, taking in the strange turn of events. Then, recovering, he said, looking puzzled,

"I'd always thought that was a girl's name, anyway."

"It's a girl's name with a double e. He'll be known as Desy."

"Well, that's unusual." He responded.

"Says the man with the strangest name I've ever heard. When are you going to tell me the truth about your name? I've never believed that rubbish about Saint Brennas or being named after a place in the south of France and all the other tales you tell about it." I said.

"The truth of it is so banal that when I was younger I couldn't bring myself to tell anyone. I suppose I thought they'd laugh so I made up all those stories about it but I don't really care now."

"So where *did* it come from?"

"My mother was called Brenda and my father was called Thomas." He revealed with a resigned sigh. "The bit in my story that's true is that they really did double the n so I'd be known as Brennas as in Brenda and not Breenas."

I tried hard not to laugh, keeping a straight face, but then we both burst out laughing.

"But just think," he said, "if I'd been a girl would they have called me something more feminine than Brennas like Thomda or something? It's crazy. My grandfather wanted to change my name but my grandmother wouldn't hear of it. She said that it was their daughter's prerogative to name her own child and although she was dead they had to honour her choice. My grandmother *did* get her own way occasionally but not very often."

"So what about your surname? The exotic Silvatori." I asked.

"Well, that's genuine too. My father was never spoken about because of my grandfather's refusal to have him in the family so everything about him died with him. I suppose I could look into it. They were possibly immigrants from years back, looking for work on Teeside."

It was time to go. He stood up, kissed my hand, and then turned to the coven, nodding his head in a gracious goodbye, almost clicking his heels. He'd gone from being a Viking to a Prussian cavalry officer. A sigh of admiration whispered through the hags.

*

I lay back and thought about my relationship with Brennas. I'd found him both attractive and annoying when I first met him. He was funny and entertaining, liked beer and bands and that seemed to be it. But then while I was living in the same house with him I gradually came to see his true nature which was gentle, generous and caring. I'd realised that my feelings for him had been changing into something more like love than liking. On the other hand, I'd dramatically fallen for Steve but in a completely different way. For Steve I'd felt what I suppose you'd call lust, something solely carnal because I knew that he didn't have a kind nature and yet I couldn't deny the electricity I felt when I was near him. But now that very electricity had barred me from the one person who I now realised I truly wanted to be with. Brennas was being very kind and caring towards me because that was his nature but I remembered the look of horror and total disrespect on his face when I told him about the baby and Steve. I was now what my mother would have called damaged goods, a slut, and there was no way out of it. I knew that if I ever let Brennas see how I felt about him he would be revolted. It would be difficult to go on living in the same house with someone I loved, knowing that it could never be reciprocated.

As for my feelings for Steve, I was reminded of something Robert Greene had said in one of his plays. I couldn't recall the words exactly as I lay there half asleep but it was something about the blooms of the almond tree growing in a night and vanishing in a morn, a fly taking life with the sun and dying with the dew, fancy slipping in with a gaze, going out with a wink. I knew then that lust is transient; love is forever and I slipped into sleep.

19

The next couple of months went by quickly in a blur of tiredness and sleeplessness. Looking back, I wonder how I would have managed if I'd been alone in a one room bedsit managing Desy and everything else that we have to do to stay alive. Marion came to give me respite whenever she could and Brennas supplied the meals or I would have starved. But would I? When there is no alternative to the situation that we find ourselves in we somehow manage so perhaps I would have coped but the fortunate part of all this is that I didn't just have to cope.

Time had wandered into May and my life was settling into a pattern, my energy returning. Brennas had finally finished the book on Adelia after so many delays. He said that was the end of the series on the lesser known poets that he'd been writing but he didn't know whether any more work would be coming his way. He was in the house a lot and seemed distracted and restless. One afternoon after a long phone call he came into the kitchen.

"That's what I'd been waiting for." He said. "That was Dottie's solicitor. The probate's finished so I have to go up there. You must come too. I'm not going to leave you here on your own. Anyway, it's a long journey and you can keep me amused." He said, glancing at me with that cheeky smile.

"But there's too much stuff to cart around." I replied, although I wanted to go, not just for the break but to be close to him.

"That's why I'm renting a car." He said, looking pleased with himself.

So that was settled and I looked forward to it. Desy slept most of the way so perhaps the motion of the car pleased him. We had to stop for his feed and a break for ourselves too but the journey was easier than I'd thought. As we got closer to the house the sadness crept in again that Dottie wouldn't be there with her enthusiastic greetings. The Thompsons had been asked to continue looking after the house and garden until all the legalities had been completed so everything was much the same but not the same.

The next day Brennas went to the solicitor while I wandered round the garden and the fields. The beauty of it and the peace made me want to leave London again. Hawthorns were bent over, so laden were they with may blossom, cow parsley skirted the paths, and huge horse chestnut blossoms towered over me. But it was the bluebell wood that stopped me in my tracks. It was more than a sea of blue, it was a deep ocean. I was carrying Desy in a kind of papoose that I'd fashioned from one of the shawls that Dottie had given me. As I walked along the narrow path through the wood I remembered a game that I'd played at birthday parties when I was a child. We would form a circle and one of the children would go in and out round all the other children in the circle who would be singing a sweet little song. When the song was over the child would tap the back of the person they'd arrived at, at that point. That child would then join the first child going in and out round the circle until eventually everyone had joined the little procession. I remembered it as having been my favourite party game. While I was thinking about it I started humming the tune and then the words of the song came flowing back as my hum turned into the song.

"In and out the dustin bluebells, in and out the dustin bluebells, in and out the dustin bluebells, my fair lady. Pitter patter, pitter patter, on your shoulders, pitter patter, pitter patter on your shoulders, pitter patter, pitter patter on your shoulders, my fair lady."

It was repetitive and I sang it over and over again as if I was the leader circling the group looking for my fair lady. When I turned round to go back I saw that Brennas had been standing watching me. He had such a tender look in his eyes. He came towards me and put his arm round my shoulders, pulling me into him, looking down at me and kissing the top of my head.

"You are my fair lady in the dustin bluebells." He said looking down at me and kissing me again but this time, not on the top of my head.

But then he quickly took his arm away and said sorry. But, because this was what I'd been wanting for so long I couldn't stop myself.

"No, please don't go away, don't stop."

We both looked at each other in a way that neither of us had dared to during those long months after my downfall, as I called it. He put his arm round me again, folding me into him.

"I've loved you from the minute I first saw you." He said.

I wanted to say that you can't love someone until you really know them as I'd learned from bitter experience but I didn't want my pedantry to spoil this unexpected yet longed for moment, a moment that I'd convinced myself could never happen because of the sort of person I'd apparently turned out to be.

"Do you think I stood next to you at the buffet at your uncle's funeral by chance? It was deliberate so that I could get to know you. As soon as I saw you I asked your cousin Pete who you were. He told me that you lived in London too but getting the same train back was actually providential. I really didn't know you'd be on it and got as big a shock as you did when we saw each other. I'd got your phone number off Pete because I hadn't expected to see you so soon after. If you hadn't gone to the club that night I'd have phoned you the next day. I had to wait a while until after you'd had the baby before I told you how I felt because you had enough on your plate and if you hadn't felt the same it would have been difficult to go on living together. I didn't want that to happen so I had to bide my time. But seeing you just now and for some other reasons that I'll tell you about, I decided that now was the right time to tell you how much I love you, have always love you."

We managed another kiss with Desy squashed in the papoose between us.

"I've loved you for a long time too." I told him. "It's been agony because I felt that you wouldn't want a second-hand woman, as my mother would have called me. If I'd made my feelings clear that would have put you in an embarrassing position and I supposed it could have ended our friendship. It's like you said, you know, if one person in a friendship feels for the other one in a way that's not reciprocated then living together, perhaps even still being friends just wouldn't have worked anymore. I couldn't risk losing you so I didn't show you how I felt."

He laughed. "A second-hand woman? Which century are we living in? Did you think I was waiting for a virgin?"

"But there's one thing I don't understand." I continued. "If you'd felt like that right from the beginning how come you never approached me?"

He looked at me for a minute as if he was working out how to say it.

"When I saw the effect that Steve had on you I knew there was no point because I'd been there before. If I showed an interest in a girl he'd make it his business to take her whether he liked her or not. He did it because he knew he could. It was childish and mean of him but it was as if he had to keep proving something to himself."

"Why did you go on living with someone and being the friend of someone who was so despicable?" I asked.

"I suppose it was just laziness." He said with a rueful smile. "We were part of the same group of friends. I couldn't bring myself to ask him to leave, I suppose, because I'd have to give a reason, oh, I don't know. I know I should have moved or asked him to move but it all takes so much time and energy when you're busy working."

We managed another kiss with Desy between us and I hoped that that wasn't a metaphor. Would Desy come between us? He would always be Steve's child, a constant reminder. But I was not going to allow anything to spoil the joy we felt at the long-last admission of our love for each other which was like the sudden relief from a burden that we'd carried for so long that it had just become part of our lives and behaviour, never allowing ourselves to express it. I thought over how strange and sad it had been that we'd both felt the same way but for different reasons had kept silent.

We went into the house and when Desy was settled we celebrated our new beginning. We sat closely on one of the deep sofas in Dottie's magical living room and talked about all the times we'd wanted to tell each other that we were in love. Brennas remembered how we'd toiled in the garden together in Kentish town, how we'd often gone out for a drink together but just as friends and how Dottie had been convinced that we were a couple although we'd kept putting her right. It wasn't until Brennas told her about the baby and how my boyfriend, as Brennas had put it, had abandoned me that she finally came to remember the situation correctly. That reminded us of that traumatic night when we'd realised that there was only one bed. We both confessed that we'd have liked to have stayed in that bed together but the timing wasn't right, it could have prematurely rushed our slowly growing fondness for each other. But tonight was not that night, it was a night like no other so although Mrs. Thompson had made up two beds as usual we went back in time and chose just one, preferring to enjoy the warmth of being together.

20

The next morning, after breakfast when all the jobs had been done and Desy was quiet, Brennas asked me to sit down because as he'd now got all the information from the solicitor concerning Dottie's estate there were some very important matters that we had to discuss. He looked very serious so I sat down and prepared to listen. The first thing he told me was that the cottage that Mr. and Mrs. Thompson lived in had been left to them along with a legacy. Even the nurse who had lived with Dottie for only a short time had not been forgotten. There were donations to charities, gifts to friends and neighbours.

"Dottie left the house to me as she'd already told me she would and all its contents and of course money too. But to you, fair lady, she has left a considerable amount of money, in fact a life-changing amount. You'll never have to worry about the future again. You will never have to go back to that Social Security office. She has also left you her Parisian clothes, all her jewellery and Henri's wife's jewellery too. You are now a lady of independent means just as Dottie was. But there's more. She has put money in a Trust for Desy. Of course, when she died she didn't know whether you were going to have a boy or a girl so the solicitor will complete that document now that he's been born and has a name. When Dottie came back to England she was very fortunate to have a friend who was a wise investor, very clever with finances. He enabled her to increase the fortune that she already had and that's why there's so much money."

Of course I cried. Dottie had known how I would be treated as an unmarried mother and how some people would be cruel even to the child too but she also knew how the world works and how an unmarried mother who was rich would be forgiven her sins. She was shielding me and caring for my child for the rest of our lives even though she was no longer here. He now reached over across the table and took both my hands in his.

"So now you're solvent for all eternity you'll have to think carefully about what you want to do in the future."

When we were in the bluebell wood saying how long we'd been in love with each other I'd presumed that we were now together, a couple. Not for the first time was I being presumptuous about what I thought a man wanted from me, was what went sadly through my mind at that moment. Then he came round to my side of the table and put his arms round me.

"I've decided to leave London and live here."

I knew now that he was explaining that we were parting. He'd expressed his love for me but that was all, it was not going to lead anywhere. He was going to lead his own life and he was expecting me to do the same. A deep sadness as powerful as the happiness I'd felt earlier overcame me. But then he continued,

"So what I'd like to do more than anything is for us to get married and come and live here together as a family. But I do understand that your life's changed now so that mightn't be what you want to do."

After so much turmoil in my life all I could do, yet again, was to cry. Why do I keep doing this? I asked myself. I don't seem to be able to have a serious conversation anymore.

"Is that a yes or a no?" He asked. "Are you crying because you're happy with the idea or because it's not what you want? Perhaps you might like some time to think about it and compare it with all the things you could do now."

I looked up at him. "You're all I want."

We kissed again as Desy made his presence felt. That reminded me of something that had occurred to me the day before. I lifted desy out of his cradle and as I nursed him I looked seriously at Brennas.

"There's one thing we have to discuss." I said. "Desy will be a constant reminder of what happened with Steve and me. If he grows up to look like Steve it will be an even more apparent, constant reminder."

"Well, although it grieves me to admit it", Brennas responded, "even I can see that Steve's very good looking; that's why all the girls fall for him. So if Desy has his looks that'll be fortunate for him. People are nicer to the beautiful of this world."

I remembered that I'd noticed that myself what seemed like a lifetime ago when I fumbled around with my silly equation of beauty in relation to Steve's skin-deep beauty as opposed to his not so beautiful nature. As if reading my thoughts, and not for the first time, Brennas added,

"One thing's for definite though, he won't have Steve's derisory attitude or caustic nature because you, or dare I say that *we* will be bringing him up. Anyway, I don't think of Desy as being Steve's I only think of him as being yours and hope that you'll let him be mine too. I'd love to be his father. I'd try to give him the life that I'd wished for when I was a kid."

Oh dear, more tears. I couldn't stop now once the dam had been breached but it was good to cry it out, a relief to let out all the bad energy that had been silting up my inner reservoir. When your widest dreams are realised it's odd that no words come, but your body demonstrates how you're feeling on your behalf.

*

When we got back to Kentish Town to pack up our London life we rounded up all our friends, the gang, as I called them, and arranged to meet them in our local as we'd done so many times before. We arranged for the babysitter we'd used before and trusted, bearing in mind how fearful I was of anything happening to Desy. We'd been away for quite a few weeks so after the greetings we told them our news. Strangely, our friends were not surprised. There were comments such as, "about time too", "so you finally got round to it", "what took you so long?" Had it been obvious to everyone but ourselves? Had they thought that Desy was Brennas' child or had they seen how well we suited each other?

A band was playing at the pub that night. I was standing, watching and listening for a while when I felt someone stand beside me and put their arm round me. As I looked up I found that I was not looking into Brennas' sapphire eyes as I'd expected to be but into the jet eyes of Steve. I lost my bearings. Wasn't he on the other side of the world? Wasn't he the last person I wanted or expected to see? What was he doing here? I spun round to release myself from his arm. He was tanned from his time in Australia which only added to the equation but my infatuation, as Brennas had called it, had long died. I felt no attraction for him. The generator had broken down.

"Hello Elfie." He said.

"What are you doing here?" Were the only words I could utter.

"That's a nice welcome home!" He laughed.

"It's not a welcome."

"Well, that's not very nice, is it?" He seemed a bit tipsy. "I'm just on a visit and thought I'd come and join you all. So the ogre finally got his elf, did he? The giant caught the fairy. Beauty and the beast."

He was recalling the joke he'd made from when he'd watched us digging the garden which at the time we'd all laughed at and yet again at Marion's wedding but this time it didn't soften my feelings towards him. He said nothing about Desy which was just as well because I wasn't prepared to talk about him. Some friends joined us and I slipped away. I found Brennas and told him that Steve had turned up out of the blue.

"I know, Nick's just told me. He hadn't told anyone he was coming. He's over on business, apparently."

"I don't want him here." I said.

"We can't really throw him out, can we, it's not a private party." He stated. "There are enough people here for you to keep out of his way."

He folded me in his arms as he had done in the bluebell wood and asked me why I would let Steve spoil anything for me.

"That shows that he still has power over you, a different kind of power than before, though, I hope." He added.

Seeing Steve again had brought back all the pain of that time; the disdain I'd had to suffer from the perfect people, his total lack of interest in what we'd done apart from his presumption that an abortion was the only answer, my fears for the future. But then it also brought back how Brennas had loved me through all of that and saying that he'd saved me both physically and mentally was no exaggeration. I cheered up but then noticed Brennas and Steve talking. I wondered what about. I was pleased that Desy wasn't here so Steve would not see what he had no right to see. I recognised that the emotions that I was feeling were resentment and aversion, dare I say even hatred? And I was saddened that I disliked my own child's father so much. When I became pregnant I certainly hadn't expected or wanted, Steve to marry me. I had only wanted him to accept the truth that he was to be a father and perhaps even to show some interest in his own child, to acknowledge him, and perhaps even to help me in some way. All he'd wanted to do was to kill the child.

When the time came to tell Desy about his biological father I knew that I mustn't let him see my distaste. I would only tell him the good things. But what were they? The haze of bitterness that pervaded my thoughts around Steve was preventing me from seeing him as a normal person. When he was safely back in Australia that distance plus time might enable me to see things differently. Brennas had known him since their days at university so perhaps he might know of something good about him. As I pondered these feelings I realised that the resentment I felt against Steve was also against myself. Just one careless moment and your life changes forever.

21

Brennas gave the landlord of that momentous house in Kentish Town two months' notice and we set about sorting through our possessions, clearing out what we no longer needed. The house was rented furnished so all we had to do was to remove our own belongings. The esoteric group of scholars from academia who were interested in Brennas' series of books asked him to give a lecture on Adelia's poetry, her relationship with Frederic, her husband, and their connection to Wordsworth. Brennas commented that the research he'd done on Adelia seemed like a lifetime ago but as we were still in London he agreed to do it. I'd have liked to have gone too but as lecture halls and babies don't mix well I stayed in Kentish Town and carried on sorting through what I wanted to keep and what to let go. There seemed precious little that I wanted to keep but it felt good, like a snake shedding its skin ready for a new life; a new butterfly realising that it could fly. It was energising.

I was looking through my old university files. Was it too early to get rid of them? Would I ever need them again? Although there seemed to be a great deal, I'd just decided to keep them for the time being when the doorbell rang. Since we'd returned to London we hadn't been going out in the evenings much because of Desy and so friends had taken to calling round and as I walked down the stairs I hoped that it was Marion.

When I opened the door the dying sunlight revealed Constantine, the Roman emperor, whose statue I'd passed in York when Brennas and I had gone up north together for the first time. I tried to hide my shock.

"Brennas isn't here, sorry." I said to Steve trying to hide my surprise and starting to close the door.

"Hang on." He said. "I know he isn't here, that's why I've come. I'd like to see my son."

"You can't see him because you haven't got a son."

"What?"

"You incinerated your son so he doesn't exist for you."

"What on earth are you talking about?" He asked, frowning.

"The only solution you could see was an abortion so according to your own choice you don't have a child."

"I have a right to see my own child."

"You don't have any rights over my child because you disowned him, wanted him exterminated."

"When you told me you were pregnant you said that I had the right to know that I was going to have a child so presumably I now have the right to see that child."

"You presume wrongly." I said.

He was still standing on the doorstep and our voices were getting louder. He looked round the street, embarrassed.

"Let me in. This is stupid."

I started to shut the door but he put his foot in the door and stopped the door from closing. That frightened me and I wondered if he was going to force his way in. At that moment Brennas came down the street and saw what was happening. He came up to us, pushed Steve off the step and stood between Steve and me, demanding to know what was going on. I'd never seen Brennas lose his temper and I didn't know what form it would take. If you saw him he would look like the sort of person that you wouldn't mess with, the sort of person you don't want to meet down a back alley although when you knew him you could see that his appearance belied his gentle nature. But I could see that this time he was riled.

"What the hell are you doing, Steve? He hissed.

Steve stepped back, his arrogant demeanour vanished.

"What are you doing here Steve?" He repeated. "I told you yesterday that I'd let you know. I had to discuss it with Eve. It's her decision. Why didn't you just wait until I got in touch with you instead of barging in like this?"

"Discuss with me?" I asked.

"Steve wants to see Desy and I said I'd discuss it with you. We haven't had chance to talk about it yet. I'll phone you tomorrow, Steve."

This time Steve didn't argue. Looking back, it was like Ragnar Lodbrok squaring up to Emperor Constantine, an impossible action according to history but if a sci fi film director decided to portray such a meeting between a Viking and a Roman then we had the actors here, ready. Brennas came into the house and slammed the door. I was shaking.

"So I take it that you don't want him to see Desy?" Brennas asked as he stood with his back to the door.

"He has no right. He wanted to kill him."

"What do you mean?" He looked horrified.

"But you know that he wanted, no, expected, me to have an abortion."

"Eve, don't think of it like that. He didn't want to kill Desy. He wanted to put an end to a cluster of cells to prevent it from actually becoming a baby."

"No, at three months it's more than a cluster of cells." I responded.

"Well, he wouldn't have known that, would he?" Brennas said.

"Why are you sticking up for him?" I accused.

"I'm not. I'm just trying to understand it from his point of view. Lots of men would have acted in the way Steve did. But there's something else. There's another point of view that you need to consider. Desy's. When Desy's growing up it'll be natural for him to want to know about his biological father. If he finds out that you prevented him from having a relationship with his real father he'll resent you for it."

Resentment. There was that word again, that viral emotion that consumes you. Was I going to allow it to proliferate out into the future, to infect other people? I could stop it now.

"You're right, Brennas. You're very wise." I said.

"So, will you let Steve see him? I know it goes against the grain, but for Desy's sake not for Steve's sake, will you let Steve see him?"

"I wish I knew why he wants to see him. He always has an agenda."

"We could ask him. So shall I call him and say he can come tomorrow?" Brennas asked.

I felt that deep fear again that I'd had in the hospital after Desy was born, a fear that something would happen to him, that he'd be taken from me. I mulled over why Steve was suddenly taking an interest.

"What if Steve wants to take him away?" I blurted out.

Brennas looked at me with a puzzled expression.

"How? Abduct him? Put him in a suitcase and take him back to Australia?"

He was laughing at the thought but then he saw the look on my face.

"No, I mean later when Desy's growing up. He'll spin exotic tales about how fabulous life is in Australia and he'll lure him out there when he's old enough. He'll do it just because he can. Just to show his power all over again."

"Do you really think that?" Brennas asked.

"He takes what other people want, you've said that yourself."

"He wouldn't want to be saddled with a son." Brennas persisted.

"But Desy would be grown up. He would have taken him from us and that would be enough for him. He wouldn't care after that."

"Imagine this." Brennas responded. "Imagine that Steve doesn't live in Australia and we don't even know where he is. Then Desy breaks the news to us that he's decided to emigrate to Australia. Right? So that would have nothing to do with Steve; it would just be a young man deciding to emigrate. I'm just trying to show you that what you fear is what could happen anyway regardless of Steve's influence."

"That hasn't helped." I said mournfully.

"You're making yourself depressed worrying about something that you have absolutely no proof is going to happen and probably won't because it's so far-fetched. You're spoiling the here and now by living in a non-existent future. None of that might happen anyway because we could all be blown off the planet by a nuclear bomb. Why don't you worry about that instead?"

Brennas was frustrated with me, this being the nearest thing to a quarrel that we'd ever had. I knew he was right. I'd worried in the hospital about Desy being called up to an imaginary war, being killed on an imaginary battle field. Did all new mothers have these feelings, I wondered? I didn't know if it was a normal reaction to childbirth but what I did know was that it was wearing me out and obviously annoying the normally placid Brennas.

"I'm sorry."Brennas said as he stroked my hair.

"No, you're right." I said. "I'm the one who's sorry."

I vowed to face this illusory, spectral future that I'd created and see it for what it was. Brennas was right; why spoil today because of a non-existent tomorrow?

"Ok." I said. We'll have Steve round tomorrow and he can see Desy."

Brennas patted my arm. "I do understand, you know." He said.

22

Steve was due in half hour and I was agitated, even though I was determined to be calm and polite. I would even offer him a coffee or, at least, ask Brennas to offer him one. Finally the doorbell rang. Brennas greeted him as if the horrors of the day before had never happened. Steve looked different, slightly nervous, his swagger not evident. I didn't bring Desy in straight away. We had coffee first to try to establish a normal scenario and calm all our nerves while Brennas asked Steve about his life in Australia. It appeared that he was doing very well in the company that had offered him the job and enabled his escape, as I thought of it. He was buying his own house near the beach and so on and on went his good fortune and the wonderful life he was now leading. But then I cut through and asked him why he suddenly wanted to see Desy when he'd shown no interest since he'd been born and certainly none before.

"It's over a year since I left and when you go to a completely different place you change somehow, you see things differently, it changes your perspective. I behaved badly when you told me you were pregnant because I was taken by surprise. I am sorry about that now, you know."

No, I didn't know and I didn't know if he was telling the truth or just trying to mollify us, although I did notice that his face changed while he was saying this. It looked fresher, more honest, as if a layer of something had been stripped away. I decided to get this over with and went to fetch Desy. As I came into the room with him, Steve stood up and came over to me. He looked down at Desy's lovely face and he smiled, reaching out his arms to take him. I hesitated but then passed him over. I hovered next to him, watching him. When I looked up, Brennas was watching, not Steve but me. Was he looking to see if he could detect whether I still had feelings for Steve? We sat down again, Steve still cradling the baby. He seemed genuinely taken with him and couldn't stop smiling. He was talking in baby language to him, something I would never have expected from this detached, cold man.

"Do you think you'll stay in Australia?" Brennas asked.

"Definitely. It's a fabulous life."

Brennas and Steve then chatted about people they knew, about us moving to Durham, their old football team, all sorts of things they had in common as if the stand-off yesterday had never happened. Desy suddenly started squirming and crying. It was time for his feed and I gladly took him off Steve and left the room. I took longer than usual because I didn't want to go back into the room. Here we all were back in the same old house in Kentish Town with Steve and Brennas arguing about football as if it were the old times, but where was I? I had the baby of one and was about to be married to the other.

Steve finally left, thanking us, apparently genuinely. He said that he was going back to Australia in a few days' time and would we meet him and the others for a farewell drink tomorrow night?

"So, that wasn't so bad, was it?" Brennas said when Steve had left.

"It was." I replied.

"What was wrong?"

"Just a feeling."

"Shall we get the babysitter and go for a drink with everyone tomorrow?" He asked.

"No." I replied. "But you go."

"I won't go if you don't go." He said with that challenging smile. "It's good to get out and have a break. Just keep out of his way if you don't want to talk to him."

So we went. As we walked along I remembered that when Steve had originally left to go to Australia he hadn't even said goodbye to me. I felt my breathing quicken which it always did when I fed my resentment. I'd promised myself earlier that I would put a stop to these feelings but they just flowed on and on. I made a vow to myself to come to terms with everything that had happened. I had no idea how to do that. The word forgiveness came unbidden into my mind. It would be forgiveness for myself. My upbringing was underneath all of this, ingrained, causing me to feel guilt because I'd broken the rule, that rule of how women are supposed to behave. As I'd noticed before, I think I was more resentful against myself than against Steve. So, how do you forgive yourself?

"You're very quiet. Is it because you don't really want to go?" Brennas asked.

"No." I said. "I was just thinking."

"Thinking's bad for you." He laughed.

How right he was.

23

Our wedding plans were under way. The marriage itself would just be a small ceremony in the local Register Office followed by a party combining the wedding reception with a farewell to our friends. Brennas asked me if I was going to get in touch with my mother and invite her to the wedding. I laughed and said that no, it hadn't occurred to me. I thought later that if I was going to try to come to terms with Steve then perhaps the time had come for me to do the same with my mother. However, If I were to go and see her should I take Desy or tell her about the baby after the wedding? She mightn't take the news so badly if, by that time, I was actually married. But then again, if I took Desy with me or told her about him she would presume that he was the child of the man I was going to marry. I supposed that it wouldn't matter if she thought that because she wasn't likely to find out the truth, was she? And I didn't have to tell her.

Now, in the twenty-first century as I look back on all this, it sounds so absurd. Some women nowadays actually choose to have a baby alone and remain single. Many people now have partners rather than husbands and wives. How could all of this have changed so radically in just a few decades? No more shame, no more blame. But that's now; this was then.

I finally decided to go and see my mother, but alone. I phoned and asked if I could go over and see her. She was, of course, very surprised to hear from me just as I would have been if she had phoned me. But I felt that she was pleased to hear from me and we arranged for me to go the following Saturday.

The question also arose as to whether to invite Steve to our wedding. His farewell drinks had proved to be premature as his company had asked him to stay on longer than anticipated. We decided that we would invite him as he and Brennas had been friends for so long, if friends was the right word.

I took the train for the one hour journey to where my mother now lived. She was of that generation where what the neighbours would think of you was the most important element involved in decision making. I was around sixteen when my parents divorced in the nineteen-sixties. My mother suffered from the shame of it because divorce was another one of those things that you were not supposed to do – it was considered to be evidence of an unnecessary failure or something even worse, depending upon the circumstances that had caused it. She'd regained her respectability when she married boring Bob Burton and left the area when he changed jobs. No-one in her new life knew that she had been a woman tarnished by divorce. She'd always followed the rules and as a result she was a woman taut with tension, edgy, unable to relax. They had married after I'd left for university so apart from a few Christmases I rarely visited. We'd phone occasionally, but we'd never been close and so had drifted even further apart. As for my father, he had left for Spain soon after the divorce and I'd never heard from him again.

I rang the bell and when she opened the door she did seem pleased to see me. She smiled and seemed more relaxed. Boring Bob was out either by design or coincidence and we settled down to chat.

"I've come to give you some news." I said.

"I thought that may be the case." She said as she poured the tea.

"I'm getting married."

Her face broke into a wide smile and she congratulated me.

"Tell me all about him. What's his name?"

When I told her his name her demeanour changed.

"So he's foreign?" She asked. "Where's he from?"

Her next question would be to ask what colour he was.

"It's a funny coincidence." I said. "He's originally from County Durham, same as us. I met him at great uncle Robert's funeral. He's cousin Pete's friend."

My mother hadn't gone to the funeral because great uncle Robert was from Dad's side of the family, as was Pete and his mother, my Auntie Jean.

"So why's he got a foreign name?" She pursued.

"It's just his family name. He doesn't know where it came from originally."

If I'd told her his family history and how much money was involved she would have dropped her suspicions immediately and thought he was wonderful without even having met him, but I wasn't going to play her game.

"What does he do for a living?"

"He's a writer, an academic writer and researcher."

She weighed the information and seemed quite pleased with it. I gave her the invitation to the wedding and made my escape. How she would behave when she came face to face with Desy, I could only imagine. He'd be at the wedding and that's when she might find out that I had a child. I would have saved her the shock of finding out in that way if I hadn't known what her reaction would be. I was not willing to go through the shaming again that I'd already suffered. I was glad to get back to the house.

"So how did it go?" Brennas asked as he passed a squeaking Desy over to me.

"Just as I'd expected." I said.

"Did you tell her about Desy?"

"Absolutely not."

"It'll be a bit of a shock for her, won't it?"

"I mightn't tell her. I might leave it for a bit. Marion's offered to be in charge of him during the wedding so Mum mightn't find out that he's mine at that point."

"So are you never going to tell her that she has a grandchild?" Brennas asked, looking bewildered.

"Oh, I don't know." I said.

I wondered why I was letting myself be guided by other people's hang-ups. If my mother didn't like it, well that was her problem, not mine.

"Yes, I will tell her. I'll tell her at the reception when there's a lot of noise so that no-one will hear her scream."

24

We wouldn't let anyone spoil our big day. On the other hand, it's not always within our power to prevent what other people might do. Our plans were now complete. The Register Office was booked for Saturday at 11.30am. This was to be the culmination of the love that had grown between us and, as such, we decided to have a day to remember. We chose a hotel in one of the leafy squares in Bloomsbury where we would lavish champagne on our friends and the only relatives we had – my mother, her husband, and cousin Pete who had started the whole thing off by inviting Brennas to great uncle Robert's funeral.

"Dottie would have loved this." Brennas remarked.

Dottie would be there in spirit though because I'd already decided to wear the Jacques Doucet dress with the diamond earrings and bracelet that she'd left me in her will. I would wear real flowers in my hair. It was to be a wonderful day. It was bound to be, wasn't it?

Friends reminded us that the bride and groom should not see each other on the morning of the wedding and so Marion and Nick insisted that Desy and I should stay with them the night before, Brennas staying at the house in Kentish Town with cousin Pete, who was to be his best man. Everything went to plan which was a good omen or so I thought and as I walked into the wedding room at the Register Office, the

Doucet dress caused a satisfying stir. Brennas and I hadn't often seen each other in finery before, apart from that toe-curling visit to the antique dealer many moons ago and Marion's wedding, so when we came together in the Register Office we looked at each other with not a little appreciation. As we said our vows I feared that my inner reservoir of tears would breach the dam again. But it held back and we were pronounced man and wife.

The reception was going well. Marion kept charge of Desy so that I could greet and mingle. My mother and Bob had come so I introduced them to Brennas. He underwent the interrogation with a good heart as I'd warned him in advance that an in-depth enquiry would take place as to who he was so that my mother could place him on her social spectrum. Some of our friends were setting up their instruments ready for dancing when, as I learned later, Steve sidled up to Brennas. My mother was sitting behind them and heard every word.

"I hope Desy will be calling you uncle and not daddy." He'd said. "A kid can't have two daddies, that would be confusing. Eve will always be his mother and I will always be his father, so don't you forget that."

"In name only." Brennas had replied. "You've done nothing for him. You don't have the right to call yourself his father. I'm going to adopt him and bring him up as my own."

"Like hell you are. Over my dead body."

"So be it, if that's what it takes." Brennas responded. "Why do you want to be known as his father when you've never taken an interest in him and won't be bringing him up? I thought we'd already been through all this the other day. It's just a power trip, isn't it? Just causing trouble. Getting one over on me like you've always tried to do. Why? I've never understood why you do it. It just seems like bloody-mindedness. You're going to try to make life difficult for us just because you think you can."

"If you think you can adopt my child, you're wrong. If the biological father doesn't want the child adopted then they won't allow it." Steve insisted.

Their voices were rising over the instruments tuning up. People started glancing over.

"If you insist on being known as his father what part are you going to play in his life? Tell me that." Brennas demanded to know.

Steve ignored the question and started to walk away. Brennas pulled him back.

"I'm warning you. Don't make trouble for us. We invited you here today in good will but I'm beginning to think it was a mistake. Perhaps you'd better go."

Steve smiled his smug smile. Pete wandered over.

"Everything alright Brennas?" He asked.

"Yes, Steve's just going."

179

Steve wasn't so foolish as to go on arguing at this point. He picked up his jacket and flung it over his shoulder.

"See you in court. Oh, and thanks for the invite." He called as he left the room.

My mother had been privy to the whole conversation. I'd been at the far end of the room and knew none of this until I saw my mother advancing upon me with thin tight lips and gimlet eyes.

"Who's Desy?" She demanded.

"I was just bringing him to introduce you." I said. "This is your grandson, Desy."

She didn't look at him.

"Are you telling me that you've had an illegitimate child? My own daughter has had an illegitimate child? This is beyond belief. And you didn't even tell me."

"I didn't tell you at the time because I knew how you'd react. I thought that if I told you here you wouldn't make a scene in front of so many people but I seem to have been wrong about that." I said.

"But as if that's not bad enough, please explain why the man you've just married should be called uncle and not daddy?"

Because I hadn't heard the earlier conversation I was confused.

"Uncle?" I repeated.

"It appears that another man has the right to be called daddy and he's not the man you've married." She seemed to be enjoying this. "So what's been going on? Have you turned into one of those young women who doesn't even know who's the father of her child? Or were you going to try and fob this baby off on Brennas? Has he married you thinking you'd had his child? Or have you been living in one of those communes where nobody knows who the father of their children is?"

Brennas had heard all of this and stood in front of my mother.

"That's enough, Mrs. Burton!" He said in a low voice. "Eve didn't tell you about the baby because she knew that this is exactly how you would behave."

"What sort of man are you that you'd make do with second-hand goods and take on another man's child? You could have done better than that." She retorted.

"How can you say that on the very day that I've married your daughter? You ask what sort of man I am. Well, I'm the sort of man, Mrs. Burton, who loves your daughter and would like to bring up your grandson. Does that answer your question?" Brennas replied.

This was only the second time that I'd seen Brennas angry yet he was acting more calmly than most would under such vile provocation. She ignored him and continued with her vituperation.

"So who's the father and why didn't you marry *him* when you found out you were pregnant? It's disgusting." My mother persisted, describing me in all the ways that I'd foreseen, unaware that the music had stopped and her piercing voice was echoing round the room.

Boring Bob became slightly less boring, attempting to rein her in and stop the tirade but all to no avail. She was in full flood of righteousness.

Again Brennas leaned over her and said as politely as possible,

"None of this is anyone else's business. Just rejoice in your lovely grandson."

But she couldn't put it down.

"How can I rejoice in my grandson, as you put it, when I don't even know where he's come from?"

Her ludicrous comments finally stopped when she stared at the door and a look of utter bewilderment came over her face.

"I don't believe it. How could you? How many more shocks have you got lined up for me today?"

We all followed her stricken gaze to see where she was looking and by the door I saw a vaguely familiar figure. It was my father, the father who I hadn't heard from in seven years. He caught sight of us and strode over, smiling. He hugged and kissed me.

" My goodness, you look amazing, Evie, beautiful. And this must be the lucky man, as they say."

I introduced him to Brennas and they shook hands as if this situation was perfectly normal.

"How could you do that? Invite him and not tell me?" My mother shouted at me.

"I didn't invite him! How could I invite him? I've never had his address or a phone number!" I shouted back.

"You didn't have my address?" My father asked, looking bewildered. "But what about all the letters and postcards and parcels I sent you? You never wrote back. Not once in all those years."

"Letters?" I muttered. "But I never got any letters or anything from you."

"Were you still at the same address?" He asked.

"Yes, I was there for the next two years and Mum only moved a couple of years ago."

We all turned and looked at my mother. It was now her turn to be embarrassed, shamed.

"You took all the letters Dad sent to me, didn't you?" I asked, wounded by the lost years and the resentment I'd felt towards him for apparently just disappearing. There's that word again - resentment, I noticed.

She bowed her head and whispered. "Yes."

"But why?" I asked. "How could you?"

She looked weary and beaten. All the acrimony and accusations of a few minutes ago had gone.

"I thought that he'd tell you how wonderful the life was in Spain. He'd describe how sunny and lovely it was to lure you away. I was frightened that you'd leave me and go and live with him."

That reasoning sounded terrifyingly familiar. This was a coincidence of emotion with my mother that I could fully understand. In my life before Desy I would not have understood such a sentiment. I would have scoffed at it. But I now knew exactly how she must have felt when the letters from Spain started to come through the letterbox. I saw again that fictitious future life that I'd imagined, the blood on the battlefields, the viruses, the loneliness, the lacks and losses of life, the wonderful life to be had in Australia, all the things that had made me mad with love to protect Desy. Yes, I understood. We'd all been quiet for a few minutes while we took on board the frailties and complications of relationships and love. My father just looked at my mother but said nothing.

Brennas ushered us to an empty table and called the waiter to bring us a bottle of champagne. The band, sensing an end to hostilities, played soft, easy, music. When we were settled, my father explained how he came to be there. He was still in touch with his sister, my Auntie Jean, cousin Pete's mother. He'd kept up to date with our news through them which is how he'd heard about the wedding. He'd had hold-ups on the journey hence his late arrival.

"So you never got my letters, Eve. You must have thought I'd abandoned you." He said. "I would never have done that."

Abandoned. Another familiar word. That was the word that Brennas had used to Dottie when he'd told her about my pregnancy. It was all becoming a bit surreal. Pete came over.

"I wouldn't have told you about the wedding if I'd known you were going to gatecrash." He said to my father. But he was bluffing because he knew that he would come.

"But I'm glad you did." I said. "We've sorted out something very important.

I asked my mother if she'd thrown the letters away. No, she hadn't, she still had them and the postcards and the parcels. She hadn't opened any of them either.

"I don't think the parcels will be much use to you now." Dad said. "The clothes will be out of date but perhaps some of the other stuff will still do."

"I still want them." I said. "I'll catch up with your years of news all in one go."

Nothing was said to my mother about what she'd done. My father didn't rail against her which he'd had the right to do. It was as if we'd all accepted her reason and we left it at that. I'd noticed that she'd finally been looking at Desy and she asked if she could hold him. This would be the breakthrough that I'd been waiting and hoping for. I passed him over and as she cradled him, looking into his eyes I watched as the love came in. They say that babies bring their love in with them. Brennas then took the opportunity of taking me onto the dance floor for one of the slow bluesy tunes which made our friends hoot and whistle. Had there ever been a party like this one? The tension that comes over a room when there's dissension evaporated. We danced, we laughed, we talked, we ate, we drank. All the people who had become part of my life were there in that room, even Dottie's spirit, shimmering through the silky folds of her dress, sparkling through her diamonds.

The buffet had been at been at lunchtime and now in the early evening, guests were saying their goodbyes, several groups planning to go out for dinner together. We were invited to join them but we were exhausted and voted to go back to the house. Pete invited my father to go and stay at his house while my mother and Bob made their way back home. Before we all parted, I arranged to meet my father the next day before he went back to Spain and I also arranged to go to my mother's the following week to retrieve seven years' worth of post from my father. Brennas and I got back to the house and collapsed onto the ancient settee.

"Well, we weren't expecting any of that, were we, Mrs. Salvatori?" He said.

In all the kerfuffle, the one thing that hadn't occurred to me was that my name had now changed. I burst out laughing.

"Eve Salvatori." I said. "Yes, I like it. Exotique!"

So, I now had a son, a husband, and I'd got my mother and father back. Not bad for a day's work.

25

We were in Paris, Brennas, Desy and me, sitting with drinks outside the Café Flore in the balmy early evening of the June time. I was wearing one of Dottie's dresses from the House of Worth. She must have been my exact size and shape when she was in her twenties. It was as new, had clearly never been worn, so perhaps she'd had it made during her last months in France, never having had the chance to wear it once she was back in the chilly north-east of England. A man at a nearby table had been staring at me intently which I thought was odd, not to say rude, considering I was sitting with a man and a baby. He eventually stood up and came over to us, begging pardon for interrupting us and introducing himself as the Director of Charles Worth of Paris. He told us that he had recognised the dress immediately as one of their early twentieth century creations and was fascinated to know how I had come by it. We invited him to join us and we told him Dottie's story, including a description of the other French designers' dresses that she had kept. He was enthralled. He told us that he was involved in setting up an exhibition on the history of fashion. Would we be interested in loaning the dresses? They would send their own expert packers and shippers and the same for returning them. He acknowledged that I would have to think it over and passed me his business card.

I reached my hand across the table to take the card and realised that I couldn't lift my hand because it seemed to be clamped down, connected to something. The lights around the café had all gone out. I heard shuffling and low voices. I then discovered that it had only gone dark because my eyes were closed. When I tried to open them my eyelids just fluttered. I tried again and this time they opened. I was in a small white room. Brennas was standing talking to a man who I didn't recognise. The Director of the House of Worth had been wearing a fawn linen suit and looked nothing like this man. And where was this room? How had I got here from the café? When Brennas looked over at me and saw that my eyes were open he rushed over, calling to the other man,

"She's come round."

Come round? Come round from where?

Brennas hugged me as best he could what with all the wires and machinery that seemed to have suddenly appeared.

"Where's he gone?" I asked Brennas.

"Who, sweetheart?" He asked gently.

"The Director from Worth. He was sitting with us. Where's his card?"

Brennas looked helplessly at the other man.

"I've no idea what she means." He said in a scared voice.

"It's perfectly normal to be confused when they first come round. The important thing is that she has come round. It will take a few days."

I thought about our lovely evening in the café and decided that I preferred it to this nasty little place. I must have nodded off and had a dream. I floated back to the café. Someone was calling my name. It sounded like Brennas but he was here with me at the café. My eyelids fluttered open again.

"Stay with me, Eve." He was saying. "Eve!"

The other man asked me how I was feeling.

"You're English." I muttered.

"Why are you surprised that I'm English?" He asked.

"We're in Paris so I thought you'd be French. Why have we left the café? It was lovely there." I whispered.

"Had you been in Paris just before the accident, Mr. Silvatori?"

"No, London."

"Do you have a connection with Paris?"

"Sort of, I suppose. A relative of mine used to live there but that was a long time ago, before our time."

I could hear the conversation in the background but I couldn't follow it. All I wanted to do was to get back to the café. Good, there it was. I settled down into the wicker chair and reached for my drink again but it was now too dark to see.

I heard the strange man say, "We must let her rest. You go home and get some sleep."

I let go and drifted off into the surrounding darkness.

The next day I awoke as if from a very deep sleep. I was hungry and thirsty but the worst thing was the headache. I must have drunk a lot last night, I thought. Then I noticed the room I was in. It was familiar – that nasty room I'd gone to after the café -bare and white. Where was I and why was I there? Then I saw Brennas asleep on a chair next to the bed but where was Desy if we were both here? I panicked.

"Where's Desy?" I shouted.

Brennas woke with a start and hugged me, crying. What on earth was going on? I'd never seen a big man cry before, I thought dispassionately. There was something nice about it but I couldn't think of the word.

"Desy's fine." He said through his tears. Your mother's looking after him at the house."

My mother? The house? What house? A succession of houses paraded across my mind. Glen Hall, Adelia's house came to mind, then Dottie's Eden

Manor. I saw the cherry tree in the little garden in Kentish Town. Where was my mother with Desy?

"How are you feeling?" Brennas asked. "I can tell you're a lot better because your eyes have life in them again."

"But where am I, Brennas. What's going on?"

"You'll be confused for a while, that's normal."

"But normal for what? I don't even know where I am."

At that point, the other man came in who I could now clearly see was a doctor. I see. I'm in hospital.

"Mrs. Silvatori, you're looking a lot better today. You might be able to go home tomorrow. It will take about ten days or so before you feel yourself again. You must rest, drink lots of water, no strenuous activity. Come back in a fortnight for a check-up or get in touch with your doctor if you have problems with balance or headaches or anything out of the ordinary before that time."

He left us alone and I asked Brennas again.

"Please tell me what's going on. Aren't we still in Paris?"

"We were never in Paris. You're in Newcastle General." He said. "You were confused because of what happened. It all happened so quickly. You must have been dreaming, like a hallucination but in your imagination."

"Tell me what happened." I was so confused I felt as if I was going mad.

"Ok. Do you remember that we packed up the house in Kentish Town and we were moving to Eden Manor?

"Yes."

"Do you remember that we arranged for our stuff to be taken up there by rail and then delivered?"

"Yes,"

Do you remember that we hired a car to drive up there ourselves?"

"Yes."

"Do you remember the journey?"

I thought back. I remembered the car and then being in Paris. There was a blank in between.

"No. The journey's gone."

"We were nearly there, on the A1. A lorry jack-knifed some way ahead of us but it slammed all the cars behind it into each other. By the time we were involved the momentum had died down so when a car slammed into us it wasn't too hard a hit but you took the impact on your side of the car. Desy and I got away with it. You've got concussion."

"You said my mother's looking after Desy?"

"I needed someone to look after him so I could be here with you. You were unconscious when they brought you in and they didn't know how badly hurt you might be." His eyes filled with tears again. "I phoned your mother, and Bob drove her up here straight away."

"Wow!" was all I could say.

I left the hospital the next day still feeling groggy and headachy. I could never have imagined that the first day of my new life would have taken such a strange turn. My mother greeted me enthusiastically, relieved that my concussion hadn't been labelled severe. I had a loving reunion with Desy and all seemed to be well. My mother insisted on staying until I'd had my check-up so that she could be sure that I was well enough to cope. We spent a lot of time talking, bridging the gaps that had broken our relationship. Boring Bob turned out not to be boring at all. He was a quiet, almost shy man and I realised that when I'd visited them he'd simply felt awkward.

One day as I was resting, that old thought occurred to me again. Happenstance or Providence? The word "accident" suggests something that isn't planned. But that accident had healed the rift between myself and my mother; had enabled me to appreciate her husband, whom I'd misjudged. It humbled me to realise how glibly I'd judged him and then treated him accordingly. So was it really just happenstance that these good things just came as the result of an accident or do I really have angels working on my behalf? Would you have to be someone important, someone who has power in the world to expect such help? Is it therefore arrogant to imagine that angels would work on your behalf? I decided not; they'll help anyone; you only have to ask, I thought as I drifted off into yet another deep sleep.

26

We were finally alone and the house beckoned to us to make it our own. The magnificent drawing room, the room that had taken my breath away when I first visited Dottie would be left as it was for no other reason than it was perfect. The slightly smaller room which Dottie had called the morning room, also at the back of the house was to be our main family living room. We would furnish that to our taste. We would make the main bedroom into our own sanctuary, the other bedrooms being sufficiently furnished for guests for the time being.

The first thing we had to do was to clear the massive closet and decide where Dottie's French dresses, hats and shawls were going to go. As we opened the door to this closet I noticed a cream and pink sundress. I walked towards it as if sleepwalking. I knew the feel of it; I knew it fitted me; I knew it was from the House of Worth. A memory was nudging away at my brain as I tried to remember the significance of that dress when suddenly the scene broke through.

"Brennas, look, that's the dress I was wearing in Paris when the Director from Charles Worth spoke to us. It's such a pity I can't find his business card but I suppose I could find their address. Do you remember?"

I'll never forget the look on his face. He put both hands on my shoulders.

"Do you mean the dream you had about it?" He asked.

"No, it wasn't a dream. It was when we were in Paris. We were sitting on the terrace at the Café Flore."

Brennas cupped my face in his hands and looked directly into my eyes as if trying to hypnotise me.

"Eve, we've never been to Paris – not together. You've never been out in that dress. There was no business card."

I stared at the dress.

"But I can remember it so clearly. It was just before something happened ……."

I felt nauseous and giddy. What was happening? Why couldn't he remember?

"I know I've worn that dress in Paris. The memory's so strong. I can feel it on my skin. I can taste and smell the coffee. I can feel the warmth of the evening. I can hear the people around us talking in French. I can remember looking at you and Desy and feeling so happy, happier than I've ever been in my whole life." I said in a rush of feeling.

He took hold of my hands. "It's still the concussion. At your check-up the doctor said it was all going well but he did warn us that it might last a bit longer. He said to go back if anything cropped up. We'll get this Paris thing sorted out, don't worry. Perhaps we should go back to the hospital so the doctor can explain it to you."

I wondered then if perhaps it wasn't concussion. Perhaps my brain was bleeding and drop by drop my life was seeping away. The thought increased my giddiness.

"So are you saying that when I thought we'd been in Paris it was just a dream? While I was unconscious?"

"That's what it was. But obviously a very vivid, graphic dream. Let's try and make some sense of it. Tell me again exactly what you thought you remembered when you first came round in the hospital."

I described the scene at the cafe to him while he listened intently.

"Do you remember when you and Dottie were trying on the clothes in the closet one afternoon? I came in and heard you both laughing?" He asked.

"Yes." I smiled at the memory.

"Did you try that dress on that afternoon?"

I thought for a moment. "Yes, I did. That's when Dottie said I must be the same size and height that she'd been in her twenties."

"So that's how you know how the dress feels. When Dottie told you about her time in France did she ever tell you any stories about the House of Worth?"

In my mind, I went back to those afternoons when Dottie and I would sit together and she would tell me all about her time in Paris and Antibes. I was enthralled, loved the stories, lived them with her as she recounted them as if I had been there with her.

"Yes. She knew the Director. He always made a fuss of her."

"And the Café Flore?" Brennas continued.

"Yes, she went there with Henri, quite often. In fact she showed me a very old photograph of them sitting there under a parasol."

In this way we gradually unravelled the mystery of my dream. Later we could laugh about my secret trip to Paris but the taste, the flavour of that dream never left me. Part of me wouldn't, couldn't, give up the notion that we had truly been in Paris that evening but I kept that to myself. Perhaps there really are parallel universes and I had slipped through the mist that divides the realities. Perhaps a traumatic experience throws us into that other life but we just call them vivid dreams. Alternatively, if we look back on another person's memories, do they then become our own memories? Our memory of their memory. Can our brains differentiate between the two?

"How do you feel now? Should we go back to the hospital?" Brennas asked.

"No." I replied. "The doctor said I'd come out of the concussion gradually, didn't he, so I'll just have to wait."

"Do you still have a headache? Are you still giddy?"

I had to answer yes to these questions. During the next two weeks I would occasionally become disorientated, standing, staring, with no idea what I was doing or going to do. My head would spin, my balance threatened, my eyes becoming vacant. When this happened Brennas would lead me to the bed or sofa and I'd sleep deeply. Then memories, or were they dreams, would befuddle my mind. Twice we went back to the hospital but each time they would say that it was all normal. Normal? Then I realised that the word "normal" was relative and could only be used in context.

This drama eventually came to its natural end, the headaches, bewilderment and dizziness subsiding. What I recognised as my own normality returned and Brennas asked me if I'd enjoyed my holiday on Alpha Centauri. We tried to pick up where we'd left off but where was that? We'd only been married for a few weeks but the wedding day seemed to be a century ago. I could never have imagined that my entry into Eden Manor to start my new life was not to be carried over the threshold but would be to stagger out of a taxi from a hospital.

But something seemed to have shifted. I felt that I couldn't make a life for myself, for us, in Eden Manor. I loved the house, but I realised that it would always be Dottie's house. I could never make it mine. The furnishings, the pictures, the mirrors, everything so perfectly fitting for the house, belonged to Dottie. Even if I stripped the house to its bare bones could I ever feel that it was mine? I would always feel like a guest in my own home. Brennas had been used to this house all his life, even knowing that one day it would be his and so to him, it was his. Was that what was at the bottom of this? That the house was his and not mine? That it held his history and not mine? That I was an outsider, looking in? How could I tell him how I felt especially as I didn't even know the real reason for the way I was feeling? Was it related to the bang on the head? I asked myself. Was I becoming deranged?

"You seem a bit down." He said. "What happened to you was traumatic. It'll take time to get over it. Anyway, there's something I need to talk to you about."

We sat at the table facing each other and as usual when Brennas had something serious to say he reached over and took hold of both my hands.

"Because this house was left to me in the will, the deeds will be given over to me in my name but I want it to be *our* house not just mine so I want your name on the deeds too so that we both own it jointly. We'll have to go to the solicitor's so that you can sign the documents but I wanted to wait until you were well enough to go."

"That's so thoughtful of you, Brennas." I said. "That would be wonderful. But there is just one thing. Would you be willing to change anything or do you want to leave everything exactly as Dottie had it?"

"Well, it's interesting that you've mentioned that because I've been thinking about it. I know we said we'd leave most of it as it is because it's so right for the house and Dottie had such good taste, a good eye. But we don't want to live in a museum dedicated to Dottie, do we? She would have hated that; she would want us to make this into our own home. But if you want to keep it as it is, I don't mind. What do you think?"

Synchronicity, coincidence, mind reading? All my misgivings fell away. This would be our home.

During the time of concussion Desy seemed to have absorbed the tension and strangeness in the atmosphere, being especially demanding and whiny. The return to normality had given back to us our lovely, cheerful baby. The next few months were blissful with Desy continuing to thrive, the house gradually becoming our own and Brennas and me having sweet afternoons in our bluebell wood with Desy asleep by our side. The passion that Brennas and I had felt for each other for so long, not daring to show it to each other but finally admitting it there, in that wood, made the memory of it almost palpable whenever we went there. It was a special place.

*

For several months after our arrival at Eden Manor we spent time exploring the area, walking the trails around the house and driving out to the sea and the hills. It was as if our lives had suddenly paused, placed us out of the reach of time. The common vexations of life were suspended as we lived an enchanted life.

We discovered that Adelia's Glen Hall was now open to the public and we decided to go down Memory Lane. When we walked in, the first thing we saw was Brennas' book for sale in the reception area. The painting of her by Edward Wansbeck had been beautifully reproduced on the front cover. At that moment, Mrs. Howard, the warden, walked through and recognised us immediately. She showed us round the newly refurbished house and then there I was, back in the library. The poignant memories of those times were folded into the fabric of the room as closely as Edward's love letters to Adelia had been folded into her books.

When we told Mrs. Howard that we were now living near Durham, not far away, she begged Brennas to come to the house once a month to give talks on Adelia, her life and poetry. It would be voluntary though, she apologised, but he could claim for petrol. I couldn't help smiling at the thought of Brennas needing money for petrol, or even me these days, for that matter. As I stood there in Adelia's library I contemplated on how unimaginably my life had changed since I was last there.

Brennas agreed to the request to give talks and when we got home the topic of what we would do with the rest of our lives cropped up. We were still too young to live a life of retirement so we discussed what to do with our time. Brennas already had friends who were working at the university and he'd discovered that there was a dearth of publishers willing to publish small arcane pieces of research, possibly only of interest to a minority academic readership. We talked over the possibility of starting up just such a publishing company which we would manage together. We started to make plans which would include turning one of the huge attic rooms into an office, the other attic room could be Desy's playroom, which could later become his study when he was ready for such things.

We lived a charmed life but we'd forgotten that when you live in the Garden of Eden you have to look out for the snake.

27

We'd forgotten about it. We didn't see it coming. The first postcard from Australia addressed to Desy arrived just as we'd settled back onto this happy even keel. It was signed "Daddy".

"How does he know our address?" I asked.

"One of the gang must have given it to him. Not all of them know the history, those who we didn't see all that often wouldn't have known. He'll have asked one of them, I imagine."

I remembered how my mother had kept my father's letters away from me. If he'd stayed in this country I could have continued seeing him but she couldn't bear the thought of him luring me abroad. This matter was different. My father had brought me up with my mother for the first sixteen years of my life. He'd had rights.

"What I don't understand," I said, "is why he suddenly turned nasty again. When he came to see Desy on his visit he seemed to have changed, explained he had a new perspective but then he flounced out of the wedding party. That was when my mother started ranting on at me. She'd overheard you and Steve arguing. Remind me what had suddenly made Steve angry again"

"He knew that I was going to adopt Desy. Although he's never claimed to be his father and has never done anything for him he still considers that he's his and so no-one else can have him even though he doesn't want him himself. That's typical of him, though. These postcards will be his reminder to us, a threat almost."

"I'll keep them and give them to him when he's twenty-one or forty or sixty. Oh, I don't know. If I give them to him as he grows up he'll be intrigued; he'll want to go and meet his father and see this fabulous place where he lives." I said.

"We'll have to make his life here with us so wonderful that he won't want to leave." Brennas responded.

The last thing I wanted or was expecting was Steve back in our lives. What I couldn't understand was why he wanted to make sure that Desy knew that he was his father but had done absolutely nothing fatherly for him, ever. But, as Brennas had once pointed out – Steve does things simply because he can, because he has the power. As Brennas and I sat across the table facing each other a stream of sunlight flowed through the window behind him lighting up his long copper-coloured hair. His brilliantly blue eyes were looking at me.

"Vike", I whispered.

He looked surprised and laughed.

"You've never called me that old nickname before."

"The Vikings never fought the Romans, different eras, but the Vikings would have won if their paths had crossed."

"Are you back on Alpha Centauri?" He asked, giving me a puzzled look.

I just smiled. I was determined to ignore Steve. I'd put the postcard away for the time being. But the postcards kept coming, once a month. Soon Desy would be able to look at them and talk about them. I was in a moral dilemma. Did I have the right to throw them away? When I'd retrieved my own father's letters and postcards that he'd sent to me after he'd left for Spain I noticed that there was always a holiday on offer, always a mention of the lovely weather, the swimming pool. Yes, I would definitely have been tempted. What if I'd gone and decided that I liked it so much that I wanted to stay? He might have suggested that it was just a holiday and persuaded me to go back to my mother. I could ask him what he'd intended. On the other hand, I'd known my father, Desy doesn't know his. It's different. Here I was again, persecuting myself with a fictitious future. If the postcards continued until Desy was eighteen there'd be hundreds of them, all describing this paradise that Steve claimed to be living in.

On Desy's first birthday there was a card and a parcel with Australian stamps. I couldn't bear to look at them but eventually I opened them. The parcel contained a cuddly koala bear which Desy latched onto immediately and which became his cuddly of choice abandoning the teddy that I'd chosen for him. I had a very childish reaction to this, as if it was a personal insult. I was letting Steve get at me from across the ocean.

Brennas had had to go into town so as I sat looking at the koalan atrocity, the massive doorknocker sounded and I walked across the hall to open the door presuming it was another birthday parcel arriving. But there he stood as if I'd manifested him through my thoughts. Steve said hello casually as if seeing him on my doorstep was a normal occurrence. He leaned on the doorpost, all beautiful arrogance.

"Aren't you going to ask me in? I've come a long way."

I was so stunned that I just stood there staring at him.

"What are you doing here?" Was all I could manage.

"It must be obvious why I'm here. It's my son's first birthday."

Desy was an athletic crawler by now and would hoist himself up against a piece of furniture and take some steps. He came whizzing into the hall and as I turned to see to him, Steve came into the house and shut the door. Brennas was out and I didn't know how he'd react, finding Steve in the house. He lifted Desy up and chatted to him as I stood by uneasily wondering what to do. The last time I'd seen him had been at the wedding when he and Brennas had argued over the adoption and Brennas had told him to leave. How would he react, coming home to find Steve here? He always kept his temper even when he was clearly angry so all I could do was to hope that he wouldn't finally lose it. I decided to offer Steve some coffee and then try to get rid of him somehow.

"Why didn't you wait for me, Elfie?" He asked as he walked towards me.

"Wait for you? What do you mean?" I replied, backing away.

"I would've come back for you eventually. I was still like a kid myself when you had Desy. You could've waited until I'd grown up. There'll always be this bond between us because we've had a child together."

"A kid?" I asked. "You were twenty-four years old, twenty-five by the time he was born! How long does it take?"

"They say that men don't mature until they're thirty." He replied. "So how about it?"

"How about what?" I asked, getting more and more bewildered and anxious.

"Marry me. Come to Australia with me and bring my child with you. We'll be the family that we already are."

"Have you lost your mind?" I shrieked, my frown of disbelief growing ever deeper. "You were at my wedding. You know I'm married. In fact, I'm married to the loveliest man I've ever met."

"Haven't you heard of divorce? Think about it. It's a great life out there. You'd love it. I can't imagine what you do out here in the sticks. You must be bored out of your mind stuck out here with the big man. I bet he even reads poetry in bed." He said, with his signature smirk.

"How dare you! I think you'd better go. Go now and don't send Desy any more postcards or anything at all."

"Whether you like it or not, Elfie, you and me, we're inextricably entwined for the rest of our lives." He said.

"No, we're not. That's not true for me." I responded.

"You were in love with me, don't you remember?" He asked, moving towards me again.

"I've never been in love with you. The brutal truth is that I had sex with you because I was drunk."

"But you used to gaze at me as if you wanted me." He said, with that mocking smile. "I only gave you what you wanted."

Degraded things - attraction, lust, whatever it was, can't ever pass for love. Transience isn't part of love, nor is an attraction to a skin-deep illusion. So yes, I had gazed at him, I admit it, I'd gazed at his surface beauty but had disliked what was underneath so according to the true definition of love, I'd never loved him.

"What are you up to, Steve? What's all this about?"

"Just reminding you."

"But why?"

Before he could answer, I heard the backdoor open and close. Brennas was back. I could end all this once and for all by telling him what Steve had just said to me but I didn't because I think Brennas would have killed him. A Viking losing his temper could cause an awful lot of damage. He looked as shocked as I'd been when he saw Steve.

"Good heavens!" He said. "Why didn't you tell us you were coming? I must say I'm surprised to see you bearing in mind what happened the last time we met."

Steve ignored that, "I'm over here working on a project for a few months and it coincided with this little chap's birthday." He said, sounding like a sane, normal person.

He talked about how well Desy was doing, sat him on his knee, chatted about Australia. I sat there, revolted, knowing that Brennas knew nothing about what Steve had been saying to me. "A wolf in sheep's clothing" came to mind as I watched him talking amicably to the man whose marriage he'd just tried to break up. I knew that Steve didn't really want to marry me, he just wanted to knock me off kilter, make me attracted to him again, make himself feel powerful, do the dirty on Brennas for some unknown reason. He must have a grudge against Brennas but I didn't know what it was. He was using me and Desy to get at him. I knew I must never tell Brennas what he'd said but it lay heavily on my heart that Steve could be so hideously manipulative even though his plan hadn't worked and never would. Then he did what he always did. Just before he went, after what could have been called a congenial chat, he kicked the dirt at us.

"I've been wondering why you gave him a girl's name." He said.

Not again, I thought. "It's only a girl's name with a double e."

"You know, he'll never get a job. He won't even get an interview when employers see that name – female and foreign – no chance. By the way, one more thing. I hope you're not still thinking of adopting my Desy." He said.

Brennas said, "But it's already done. I'm legally his father."

"What?" Steve looked furious. "As the biological father on his Birth Certificate I had the right to be informed and I had the right to refuse, which I would have done. I'll take you to court."

"I'm afraid you'd lose." Brennas said calmly. "We were told by the lawyers that if the biological father has abandoned the child then he doesn't have the right to refuse an adoption."

"How dare you take my child."

Just as he'd had to say at the wedding, Brennas said, "You'd better go."

"I won't let this drop. You can't do that." He shouted as he left the house.

Desy's first birthday and here we were, me in tears and Brennas, angry.

"Come on." He said. "I know what'll calm us down."

He carried Desy, took my hand and we walked to our bluebell wood behind the house where we strolled along the narrow paths. I started to hum "In and out the dustin bluebells." We looked at each other and smiled. Would we be persecuted by Steve for the rest of our lives? There seemed to be no end to his intrusion.

28

Durham Fields 1989

For the next seventeen years Steve sent Desy birthday presents, Christmas presents and more postcards but Brennas and I neither heard from him nor saw him again during all those years. He dimmed into the past only intruding when a present or postcard arrived. When Desy had his eighteenth birthday we were on the edge of not just a new decade but after one more decade it would be a new millennium. We'd lived a blessed life these last seventeen years since that memorable first birthday, Brennas, me and Desy, close and together. Desy had grown into the image of Steve, as if I'd had nothing whatsoever to do with his conception. I didn't mind too much because, as Brennas had once said, there was no denying that Steve was very good looking and as we know, the rest of the world is lenient towards the beautiful, whether this is earned or not. Fortunately Desy hadn't inherited Steve's arrogant, caustic gene. He had, in fact, absorbed Brennas' nature, having his caring, gentle attitude and light-hearted view of the world. I was the one who had to do the worrying for both of them.

While he was growing up I'd given him the postcards and presents that kept on coming from Steve, telling him that they were from a relative. When he was told about the birds and the bees I took the opportunity of telling him that I was his mother but Brennas was the person who was looking after him just like a father, but wasn't his father. At that point he was too young to figure out that mummy must therefore have done the birds and bees stuff with another man. That came later. Eventually Desy, or "Des" as he now liked to be called, knew the story but not in any detail, for instance, not that his true father had abandoned him. I didn't give him a time-line so he just knew that his real father had gone to work in Australia.

Desy, as I still called him in my mind, was doing his A levels and started to amass university prospectuses. He'd been very keen on maths and the sciences which surprised us as the house had always been full of literature, art and music. He finally decided what he wanted to do and broke the news to us that he was going to apply to do engineering. He mistook the look of horror on our faces and laughed. Is engineering an inheritable gene? I remembered that day, twenty years ago, in the garden in Kentish Town when Steve had pronounced his profession as being of use to the world whereas according to him, Brennas was just wasting his time.

We were planning a huge party for his eighteenth with our old London friends, the friends we'd made over the years in Durham, all Desy's own friends and our only relatives who were my mother and Bob, Pete who was now married, his wife and his two daughters. I invited my father too to come over from Spain where he was still living. This time I was able to warn my mother that he was coming.

It was unusually warm for April and in the early evening some guests were scattered across the lawns, some were in the massive drawing room where loud music, talking, laughter, the tinkle of glasses could be heard. I looked across at Brennas with his halo of deep golden hair. Even from a distance you could see that his eyes were startlingly blue. I smiled to myself. He was still the Viking. He looked over and caught my eye. We smiled and held each other's gaze for a few moments.

The air suddenly seemed to freeze. A figure had appeared at the door, the vision paralysing the room with amazement. It was as if Desy had come back from the future to look in on his own party. A tall man was standing there wearing a dazzlingly white shirt which enhanced his deep tan and jet black hair. There was a possessive arrogance in his stance as he surveyed the room. He could have been Desy's twin, but born twenty-five years earlier. Since we'd moved to Durham no-one knew that Brennas was not Desy's father. We hadn't hidden it; it had just never come up. People must have accepted that Desy got his physique from Brennas and his dark hair from me if they'd thought about it at all.

There was no mistaking that this stranger was Desy's father. He couldn't even have been his uncle, so alike were they. I looked at Brennas in panic. The room had still not recovered from this strange sight, everyone standing gaping. All I could hear was the music. Loud and clear came the lyrics as Brennas walked towards Steve as if in slow motion. I heard snatches of it as I felt the ground slipping away from me:

"He's a cold hearted snake, look into his eyes. He's a lover boy at play. He don't play by the rules. Girl don't play the fool. He could only make you cry. He's as cold as ice. Stay away from him."

How ironic, I thought, that those words were being sung as Steve stood by the door. If it had been a film it couldn't have been better orchestrated. The message was over eighteen years too late except if I'd heeded it I wouldn't have the lovely Desy. Strange.

As Brennas and Steve stood talking in the doorway the tableau of guests started to move again, voices were heard, tinkling glasses resumed. I could see Desy sitting on the lawn with a circle of friends. He mustn't meet his father for the first time in public. I slipped out and asked him to come in for a minute.

"What is it, Mum?" He asked.

When we were out of earshot I said in a staccato rush,

"Something strange has happened. Prepare yourself for a shock. Your father's arrived from Australia. We didn't know he was coming."

He looked entranced. "Really? Wow! I can meet my real father?"

That hurt but I knew he didn't mean it badly. I'd always known he'd have an interest in knowing his "real" father although, thankfully, he'd never asked much about him.

"Go into the morning room through the French windows and I'll bring him in."

Fortunately Brennas and Steve were still at the door. Steve walked towards me, put his arms round me and kissed my cheek before I could stop him. I stepped back and told him to come with me and I asked Brennas to come too.

"Desy is waiting for you in here." I said as I opened the door.

The two men, called such because I realised that at eighteen, Desy was now officially a man, no longer a boy, these two men stood facing each other looking at their mirror image. I didn't need to introduce them.

"The last time I saw you was on your first birthday. You've changed a bit." Steve said, smiling.

"I'm pleased to meet you at last." Desy said, obviously at a loss as to what to say on such an occasion.

But then Steve walked towards him and enveloped him in a massive hug, then stood back with his hands on his shoulders, looking at him as if sizing him up.

"You're a great looking guy, Desy. We did a good job making this one, didn't we?" He said looking at me.

I was outraged, nauseated, that he could allude to that in front of my son and my husband. I couldn't look at Brennas or Desy. The song rang through my mind "He's a cold hearted snake, look into his eyes. He's cold as ice." I wanted him out of the house.

"We've got a lot of catching up to do." Steve said.

"Yes, we have." Desy replied, looking mesmerised. "Thank you for keeping in touch with the postcards and presents."

I was annoyed with myself for raising Desy to be so polite because he really just needed to tell Steve to push off. But, of course, Desy didn't know the history around this. Desy would imagine that Steve and I had been together and then we'd split up. Later I would have met Brennas and married him. That all sounded fairly normal. Would Steve tell Desy more than I wanted him to know? How could I get Steve out of the house because we knew that "He don't play by the rules."

"I'm keeping you from your party", Steve said.

"No, that's ok." Desy said. "It's not everyday you meet your father. What shall I call you? Dad's called

Dad, I can't ever change that." He looked lovingly at Brennas.

"That's something we'll have to discuss." Steve said as he put a hand proprietorially round Desy's shoulder.

Desy then looked at Brennas and me, not knowing what to do next, out of his depth.

"I'll get you a drink." Brennas said. "You'd better come through unless you'd like to stay in here, have some time together for a bit, away from the noise."

"What do you think, Desy? Shall we have a chat in here for a bit? Steve asked.

They decided to stay there for a while to talk and get to know each other. Brennas was about to leave the room but I was determined to stay. But Brennas motioned to me with his eyes that we should leave. So against my better judgement, I left them to it.

"He doesn't have the right", I started to say.

Brennas put his arms round me and folded me into him as he always did when I was upset. My cheek was against his chest, feeling his heart beating.

"We'll have to deal with this as best we can, for Desy's sake." He said. "I know it's unbearable and we'll just have to try to put right any damage Steve does."

"You know that Paula Abdul song, "Cold Hearted" that's just been playing? " I said, " "He's cold as ice.

Stay away from him." It could have been written about him. He'll do the same to Desy, even though he's his own son."

Later the two of them emerged and after getting themselves a drink, settled in a corner where they chatted with such animation I wondered what they could possibly be talking about. I had a close relationship with Desy and felt sure that he'd tell me. Time went by but I couldn't relax. The music carried on, there was laughing and talking, dancing, but I was back in the Alpha Centauri days of my concussion, watching it all as if through a pane of glass.

Then the air seemed to thin and brighten. I suddenly realised that he'd gone and Desy was sitting with his friends again. I'd been out of the room for half a minute and he'd disappeared. Had he really been here? I remembered that when I'd had concussion I'd passed into parallel universes, or so I'd liked to think. I thought it must have just happened again.

The friends who'd been staying the night with us left after breakfast for their long journeys home. At last I could find out what Steve had said to Desy. But Desy got there first he was so full of it. He was so excited as he gave us his news.

29

"Did you know that Steve was an engineer? Isn't that weird that I want to do that too and I didn't even know that's what my own father did out of all the jobs in the world?"

He didn't wait for us to reply.

"He's had this brilliant idea. He's the director of a big engineering company and he said I should defer my university place for a year and go and work with him to get some insight and experience. Isn't that fantastic?"

No, it certainly wasn't fantastic. So my number one fear had come about. He was going away to Australia, the other side of the world. Steve had successfully lured him away from me. Which old fear was coming next? A war? Conscription to the battle field? I felt sick. I heard Brennas suggesting that he should get some more details before making up his mind.

"No, you can't go." I blurted out. "I hoped I'd never have to tell you this about your own father but he's not a nice person. He uses people, manipulates them. I don't want him to treat you like that."

"Mum, he was really nice. But I can understand why you feel like that. When people split up there's bound to be resentment and dislike."

We were having the conversation that I'd forecast all those years ago, the one that Brennas had called my fears of a non-existent future. Well, it had come, it existed.

"Your mum's right though, Des." Brennas said. "I first got to know Steve when I was the age you are now and we lived in the same house for years. He really isn't a very nice person."

"You're just jealous." Desy sniped. "You're jealous because he had Mum first and had a baby with her."

Brennas stood up so quickly his chair fell over. He towered over Desy, shouting,

"Don't you ever dare speak to us like that again."

This was so unlike Brennas that it scared us both and we sat in silence. Just one evening in Steve's company and we were at each other's throats. Desy was behaving in a way he'd never behaved before. What on earth would he be like after a whole year with Steve? He would come back arrogant, unrecognisable. Added to that, Brennas had never shouted at Desy before. How did Steve do it? Even when he wasn't present, his malign influence held sway. My inner dam was breached and I cried which seemed to be my default position when matters became unspeakable, whether through joy or sorrow. Desy got up to leave the room but Brennas stood in front of the door, not allowing him through.

"A young man who makes his mother cry is not the sort of person I thought you were. Just one evening with your father and you've turned into this nasty person that I don't recognise."

Desy went back to the table and sat with his head in his hands.

"I'm sorry. I was just so disappointed. It seemed such a brilliant opportunity. Sorry, Dad. Sorry, Mum."

I'm sorry too, Des." Brennas said. "I've let Steve get to me. You see, this is exactly what he's like."

They both looked at me and I smiled through my snivels.

"Ok, let's talk about this sensibly." Brennas said, "because it is an opportunity, you're right. Get some more details from Steve about what the work would be, where you'd live etc. and we can discuss it."

Desy was overjoyed with this and went out humming "Waltzing Matilda."

"Eighteen years ago I told you this would happen." I said. "How can we stop it?"

"We can't. He's eighteen. All we can do is reduce the risks."

*

A large envelope arrived addressed to Mr. Desiré Salvatori. I thought how strange it was that my little boy was now *Mister.* It was a formal internship contract from Steve's company for a period of nine months. A gestation that this time Steve would witness and I would not.

"It's all above board, then. Not just Steve's sudden whim with no substance behind it." Brennas remarked.

A letter to Desy from Steve arrived separately. There was a house rented by the company for four interns but Desy would live with him until there was a vacancy in the house. There was no information addressed to Brennas and me but I had to remember that Desy was now of age and I had to stop thinking that I was still in charge of him although secretly I knew that I still was, or liked to think that I was.

It was summer. Desy had left school for good and was waiting for his results. Needless to say that he did very well, as he'd been expected to do and successfully deferred his university place to the following year. It was now just a case of getting what he needed, packing and going to the airport. We were more than astonished when Steve sent Desy the airline tickets.

"That's not like Steve." Brennas said. "Do you think he could have changed?"

"I've told you before. He always has an agenda." I repeated. "There's only one reason why he'd be nice to Desy and that's to take him away from us. I wonder how we can warn him."

"We can't do that." Brennas said.

Well, I can, I thought. When Desy and I were in his bedroom deciding what he should take I broached the subject.

"Desy, you know that I told you that Steve isn't a very nice person? He always has a reason for doing something, a reason that'll bring him out on top. He can be very manipulative in a clever kind of way, a way that you never see coming. I just want you to be aware of that. Dad and I have had a lot of trouble from him here and there and I don't want you to get caught up in it."

"But what could he do? What kind of thing do you mean?"

"He might persuade you to stay in Australia."

There, I'd said it.

"But Mum, I've got a place at university. I'm not going to throw that away."

"There are universities in Australia."

"But you and Dad aren't in Australia. I'd miss you. I'm going to miss you anyway for nine months. I'll really, really miss you. It's ages since you saw Steve. You don't know what he's like now. When I was talking to him at the party he wasn't at all like you describe him."

"He didn't even say goodbye to me when he left your party. He turned up unexpectedly and then just vanished." I said.

"But that's because his taxi was waiting to take him to the station. His flight was the next day, he had to get back to London. He looked for you to say goodbye but we didn't know where you were."

"He'd come all the way up here to see you just for a couple of hours?"

"He was over here on business and it coincided with my birthday. The problem was that it was the day before he had to fly back but he still came."

"You will write to us and phone us regularly, won't you?" I said, changing the subject.

And so I wittered on which Desy bore with his usual grace, all the agitation of the day after the party long gone.

Later, as I thought over what Desy had said, it occurred to me that he was right. I hadn't had a proper conversation with Steve for seventeen long years, the last time being Desy's first birthday when Steve had turned up unexpectedly with his mendacious suggestion that I could go away with him and thinking that he could refuse Desy's adoption. I hadn't had chance to speak to him at Desy's eighteenth so perhaps he was right and I don't actually know Steve anymore. So why didn't I realise that people can change over a period of seventeen years? Why was I keeping Steve stuck in the past, preserved as the selfish, arrogant young man, like a fossil sealed in amber. Steve was by now heading for his mid-forties.

He'd lived on the other side of the world, working for over twenty years. Why did I still think of him as the caustic, cold-hearted young man of the old days in Kentish Town? I should have let Desy meet him with an open mind.

30

Desy gave us one last wave and blew us a kiss as he disappeared into Security at the airport. We had something to eat in one of the cafés and then sat reading the newspapers to pass the time until his plane's departure. Three hours later, we stood at the airport window and watched the massive plane take off. My heart was beating so madly I thought it would break through my chest as I willed the plane to stay in the air.

"How on earth do they take off and then stay in the air?" I wondered aloud.

As we walked away, Brennas gave me the scientific explanation of how they do it but I wasn't listening. I was mentally on that plane with Desy sharing both his excitement and apprehension. We were silent on the drive back until Brennas said,

"I know what'll help. We'll go and visit him when he's half-way through his internship. We can start planning it straight away. We can go travelling while we're there, see a bit more of the place. Desy'll be allowed holidays, presumably, so we can all go off together."

I'd already thought of that and that's what we started planning to do which eased the pain a little. Desy wrote to us and phoned regularly which also helped. It turned out that after a bewildering start he'd found his feet and was enjoying it. He was now in the rented house with three other interns and seemed to be having the time of his life. Steve still took him out for a meal once or twice a week but he didn't see much of him at work. He reported that no-one had known that Steve had a son and he'd caused quite a stir when he turned up with him on his first day. There were no reports of Steve behaving badly in any way, no complaints at all.

We were now into yet another new decade. 1990 had arrived with Desy on the other side of earth but after he'd been away for around six months, Brennas and I followed up on our plan and arrived in Australia. We were surprised to see not only Desy waiting for us but Steve too. I couldn't stop hugging Desy while Steve shook Brennas' hand and then kissed me on the cheek. He told us that he was taking time off work so that he could show us around. He was very chatty and friendly, not the Steve we knew.

One day later in the week when we were getting acclimatised and recovering from jet lag we were all walking by the waterside together. Brennas and Desy went to one side to look at something which left Steve and me alone.

"Desy's a great guy." Steve said. "You and Brennas have done a really good job. What a credit to you." Then he paused and looked straight at me. "He reminds me of Brennas such a lot in his manner and personality. He's got exactly that same calmness; he never gets riled or impatient. He's always cheerful. It's that sort of charm and empathy that Brennas has. Desy must have learnt all that from Brennas while he was growing up because his personality is identical. Personality's obviously not genetic because he certainly didn't get that magic formula from me. If it was genetic, or if I'd brought him up, he'd have turned out to be a nasty piece of work."

I wondered if I'd gone into that parallel universe again. Desy had been right. I didn't know Steve anymore. Could this really be the vain, arrogant Steve talking, the one I'd kept in aspic over all these years, constantly feeding him with my resentment? Did I now have to accept that people do change, experiences mount up, perspectives alter?

He went on, "There's something I must tell you. It won't make things right but perhaps it'll help to explain things from all those years ago. Being in Desy's company was so like being with Brennas in those London days that it took me back to that time and I wondered why I was enjoying Desy's company so much whereas when I was with Brennas there'd always been some kind of friction between us. I realised that I'd actually been jealous of Brennas. I used to think it was because he was well-off, that he could do absolutely anything he wanted with all that money but I realised then that it wasn't that. It was because wherever he went, whoever he met, everyone loved him. While I've been with Desy I wondered what it was that made him so likeable and I realised that he has exactly that same quality so now I'm glad of it, not envious."

I looked at him to see if there was that mocking sneer but the expression I saw was the same as when he'd looked at Desy for the first time when he was newly born. It was if a veneer had been stripped away, leaving his face fresh and new. I had no idea how to respond to what Steve had said. It was a confession, almost an apology.

"You know, so many people have congratulated me on how lovely my son is but in all honesty I have to say to them that that's down to his mother and his step-father. I can't take any credit for it."

I felt that I should give him something in exchange for this eulogy.

"But you gave him his good looks. He'll be ever grateful to you for that."

He looked at me in amazement and then slowly we both smiled at each other and I felt the dissolution of years of fear and loathing that I'd felt towards him. We were standing under a tree at that moment and I could have sworn that I heard the whisper and soft applause of the Dryads rustling through the leaves as they witnessed the straightening of a crooked path. Do they have Dryads in Australia? I pondered inconsequentially.

Brennas and Desy rejoined us and we strolled on along the harbour, the three old housemates and their child; Steve the physical father, Brennas the spiritual father and me. Where do I fit in? I'm just the one who miscalculated the equation of beauty one moonlit night under a cherry tree, a miscalculation that nevertheless brought a beautiful boy into the world.

31

We were back home from Australia, having parted from Desy yet again. I was leaning on the terrace balustrade overlooking the lawns and distant woods, pondering the various futures that may have been my life, or my parallel universes as I thought of them. They were all rooted in the fact that I'd moved into that house in Kentish Town a life-time ago.

The first scenario I envisaged was that each of us, Brennas, Steve and I would each have led separate lives, not interacting with each other apart from being housemates. Then possibly I would have met someone or not, married them or not, had children or not, changed profession or not, whatever. Impossible to guess with that scenario.

The second idea was that Steve and I would have married due to societal pressure. He would have been filled with resentment that at such an early age all his hopes and dreams of what he'd wanted to do in life would have been shattered and as a result he would have laid all the blame on me, growing to hate me for tying him to a life of domesticity. Desy would have picked up on this and grown up to be a carbon copy of his father.

Thirdly, I imagine not falling for Steve under the cherry tree, and Brennas and I gradually falling in love, as we did, and marrying. But then I wouldn't have had the lovely Desy.

So, clearly, all in all, the life that I have actually had is the best of all possible lives and I felt the truth of that. As I came out of my reverie I noticed that Brennas was standing watching me.

"Welcome back." He said. "You were miles away. Where've you been? Back on Alpha Centauri?"

"I was looking through all the potential multiple universes that I might have lived in." I answered.

"I love it when you say stuff like that." He laughed.

"What do you mean?"

"Because you've got a weird side to you and I like it." He responded, still laughing. "Which universe have you chosen out of all the choices?"

"Only the one with you in it." I said. "But it would have to have Desy in it too so it's a bit complicated."

"Prove it to me. Tell me how much you love me. Do you love me as much as the distance from here to Alpha Centauri and back?" He asked.

"Much further." I said. "Further than the farthest star and beyond that."

That's a childish game we used to play, imagining the greatest distances possible that our love could extend to until we finally arrived at infinity. We still acted like love-struck teenagers and putting our arms round each other we went back into the house.

"I still can't get over how much Steve's changed." Brennas said. "He was positively likeable. Do you think it's possible? Was he being nice because Desy was there and he wouldn't want him to see what he's really like?"

"No, it's genuine." I said. "He's finally grown up. He suggested to me once that men don't mature until they're thirty. He's forty-three now so he's had thirteen years practice."

I reminded him of what Steve had said to me that day by the harbour and how I'd felt that he was telling me the truth.

"I suppose it is years since he last troubled us." Brennas commented. "That was when he turned up on Desy's first birthday, but when he turned up at his eighteenth he didn't do anything nasty, did he, apart from that tactless remark about you and him doing a good job. When we found out that he'd offered Desy an internship in Australia we thought that he was up to his old tricks again but that was genuine. Desy said he only offered him a trip to Australia when he'd discovered that he wanted to do engineering. When we were over there, Steve told me that too. He said that when Desy told him he wanted to be an engineer he realised that it would be such a great opportunity for him that he couldn't resist offering it to him. He said, as well, that he realised that he should have spoken to you and me first to see what we thought of it. It's odd how much he's changed but I think you're right, he's simply grown up, matured over the years."

We carried on musing over the change in Steve who'd been our bugbear for so long. I'd been so protective of Desy and so resentful over Steve's refusal to accept him that perhaps I'd gone overboard in my dislike for him. Could his behaviour really just have been the result of immaturity? A child lashing out? I didn't voice these thoughts. It all seemed so long ago now.

"It'll be interesting to see what Desy has to say about it all when he gets back." Brennas said.

32

Homecomings are sweet for those who are beloved; sweeter still for those who await them. A king returning from a triumphant campaign could not have had a more joyful reception than when Desy appeared, walking through Arrivals at the airport. All the way home we talked and laughed at his anecdotes, listened seriously to his observations, bathed in his return. Over dinner in the evening, Brennas raised the question.

"So, did Steve ask you to go back and work there after university?"

Desy looked shocked. "No, he can't do that. In fact he warned me that if I ever did want to work there I would have to go through the usual process. He said that in the case of an actual job he couldn't pull any strings. It always has to be the right person for the job. But I wouldn't want to work there anyway. It was a great experience and I'm glad I've got to know my father properly. I don't think Australia would suit me for the long term."

Brennas and I exchanged relieved glances. My years of fears over Steve poaching Desy were finally laid to rest, along with all the other thoughts I'd had around Steve.

"I wonder why he never married." I wondered.

"He told me once." Desy said. "We were out having a drink and he started telling me stuff. He said he couldn't do commitment so although he liked to have girlfriends he wouldn't ever marry. He said that when he took time off work he always went travelling; that was his favourite thing so he never wanted to get tied down."

I remembered him telling me all those years ago that if he'd had as much money as Brennas he'd have gone travelling. I can still remember the wistful look in his eyes when he said it. I was happy for him that he was now able to do it.

Desy would be going off to university in a few months' time. I was glad that he wasn't going to London. There were too many ghosts there. Each time I visited him I would relive my own time there instead of enjoying Desy's own new life, although I know that sounds selfish. It is said that you should "forgive and forget" and yes, we can forgive, although it's hard, but we can't always forget, because what has happened to you is part of who you are. We can't close our minds when a disturbing memory slides in from nowhere. It's the same as when we hear a conversation going on near to us. We don't want to listen but we can't close our ears. We can eventually accept what happened in the past but some wounds leave too deep a scar to be ever truly forgotten. The scar tissue from what happened under the cherry tree and the subsequent difficulties all those years ago still hurts sometimes when its memory is rubbed. The Philistines and

Pharisees still come out to play sometimes to haunt me.

I stood, leaning on the terrace balustrade again, that favourite place for musing. I remembered Brennas telling me that he'd loved me from the first time he saw me at great uncle Robert's funeral and I wondered why he had still gone on loving me even after he'd discovered what had happened between me and Steve when he was away in Newcastle; when I'd turned out to be just another shallow person, just another moth flying into the light and getting burned. The Viking had stayed true and loyal. I then went off on one of my tangents; into one of my inconsequential ponderings - those weren't the sort of adjectives you'd normally use to describe a Viking, were they? I wondered what Vikings were really like …..I jumped with shock as I realised that Brennas was standing beside me. I hadn't heard him come over. When I'd had concussion Brennas teased me about being on Alpha Centauri and he still used that analogy when he caught me deep in thought, so deep that I would be startled when he spoke.

"You're spending more time there than on planet Earth at the moment." He commented. "What is it? Are you worried about Desy going off to university?"

"I've gone back to 1970 and 71 and I don't know why." I replied. "I can't get it out of my head. It's there all the time like being down a mine but I don't know what I'm digging for."

I didn't understand why I was back there because I didn't like revisiting those years. I could smell and taste 1970 and 71. I could hear the music, see the faces. I could replay conversations as if they'd happened yesterday, feeling the emotions again. I had flashbacks that looked like the stills outside a cinema advertising the next film.

Later Brennas said that he'd come up with a theory as to why I'd gone back there.

"1970 and 71 were really difficult years for you. There was fear and anxiety, death, betrayal, blame, all sorts of nasties. I think that Desy going over to Australia and the fear that he'd stay there, then us going over there and meeting up with Steve again, all of that has brought up the same emotions that you felt then and your mind has linked the two events. Just seeing Steve again would be enough to take you back there, surely."

That could have been right until a few weeks later I realised that it was a physical memory. It was my body that was reminding me of 1970. When we got married Brennas and I had decided not to have children. We'd felt that we were already full up with Desy, each other, our new home, travelling and then later on our new business. There was no room for anything or anyone else. During the weeks leading up to Desy's departure to university I'd been feeling sick every day, Brennas telling me not to worry so much, making myself ill. He's only going to Glasgow, he'd say. He'll be back every weekend with his washing. I didn't reply because I needed confirmation that what I suspected was true.

When it was confirmed that I was indeed pregnant, I realised that yet again I was going to have to tell a man who didn't want a child, that he was going to have a child. I was forty-two by then and Brennas was forty-four. By the time this child was Desy's age I would be sixty and Brennas would be sixty-two. I almost laughed at the thought. More laughable still was that Desy would be thirty-seven by then but at least the child would have a big brother, old enough to be like a young father to him or her.

I chose the moment of revelation carefully. At the end of the day Brennas and I would still quite often stroll round the gardens and the wood and so it was there in the bluebell wood that I gave him the news.

"I wondered when you were going to tell me." He said. "I've been back in 1970 too because you were behaving like you were then and what was happening suddenly dawned on me."

He folded me into him in that old way of his and I could feel again his heart beating against my cheek. This was such a strange turn in our lives, so unexpected. Many moons had risen and set since those days when we'd decided not to have any children. It appeared that we'd been given the opportunity to change our minds, and our little girl, who'd been waiting for so long, couldn't wait any longer to be with us. After dinner that evening we broke the news to Desy.

"What! You mean you two are still at it?" he exclaimed incredulously and then looked quickly at Brennas expecting to be shouted at for being rude.

But no, we all laughed.

For the next six months Brennas and I lived together alone in the house for the first time since we'd married nineteen years ago until we were then joined by Adelia Dorothy. We were at the beginning of a new life again.

Is it better not to plan your life? I asked myself. I looked back at my own unplanned life. I'd been a leaf in the wind blown here by coincidence and there by providence. Now that I can look back and see the big picture from a distance, I am able to see which kind of coincidence started working with me all those years ago. It was the waft of wings not the sniff of sulphur.

Printed in Great Britain
by Amazon

45366792R00147